Orlando

Channing

Tyrone

Sylvester

THOSE KIDS NEXT DOOR!

Beyonsay

Ma

Arthur

Margaret

The right of Alan Stott to be identified as the
Author of the Work has been asserted by him in
accordance with the Copyright, Designs
and Patents Act 1988.

Published by
Candy Jar Books
Mackintosh House
136 Newport Road, Cardiff, CF24 1DJ
www.candyjarbooks.co.uk

ISBN: 978-1-912535-75-0

Edited by Shaun Russell & Keren Williams

Printed and bound in the UK by
4edge, 22 Eldon Way, Hockley, Essex, SS5 4AD

CITY ECHO

The voice of the people

PROBLEM FAMILIES. COUNCIL MUST ACT
FAST. PROTESTS OUTSIDE TOWN HALL.

There were protests today over the way the
council has handled certain problem families
in the city. Hundreds of protestors travelled into
the city centre with home-made placards to show
the council that more should be done to tackle
the problem.

NOISY NEIGHBOURS

The huge crowd of people vented their anger for
most of the day outside the Town Hall. Many had
come in early to try to discuss the situation with
councillors as they arrived for the council
meeting. They were protesting about noisy
neighbours, nosy neighbours, damage to
property, bullying and name-calling.

Many councillors avoided the protestors by
sneaking into the back entrance of the Council
House.

1

RESIGN

There were shouts of 'Sort it out or resign!', 'Get a grip!', 'End this fiasco!', 'Protect innocent citizens!', 'Down with nuisances!', 'We don't like problem families!', 'Get this sorted, *now*!', 'We don't like troublemakers!'

The shouting and protesting continued non-stop throughout the day until the Lord Mayor, Mrs Dulcie Tones, came out onto the balcony overlooking the square and addressed the people. She told them that the council was taking the matter very seriously and were working on a plan to sort it out.

CRACKDOWN

'There will be a crackdown,' she told the crowd. 'We are not going to take this lying down. We are working hard and doing everything in our power to eradicate this scourge. Troublemakers *will* be brought to justice.' Most of the crowd began to cheer and clap and there were shouts of 'About time too!'

'I'll believe it when I see it,' said Mrs Mona Lotte. Her friend, Florence Mildew said, 'There's too much of this sort of trouble nowadays. I just hope the crackdown works.'

REPORTER VERITY RUSSELL

CHAPTER ONE
Ring of Fire

Mrs Grumpold was quite elderly and, since she retired, she had put on a bit of weight. Well, quite a lot of weight, actually. All right – **A HUGE DOLLOP OF WEIGHT!**

All over.

She had big, floppy, bingo wings and her body got wider as it went down. Her legs were like small tree trunks.

Because of her size, Mrs Grumpold often became a little breathless when she did any physical activity such as walking, cooking or going upstairs.

She could not bend very easily to put her shoes on and she did a sort of **WADDLE** when she walked. Mrs Grumpold's hot pink slippers fitted her feet beautifully except for the heels which were **FLATTENED** because she could not get down to put them on properly. She could not get her heels into them, so they were more like mules now.

But, Mrs Grumpold was always happy and smiled a lot. She had many friends at the Women's Institute where she spent much of her time. She did not like going out much and would give children fifty pence if they ran an errand for her to the shops. Everyone loved Mrs Grumpold. Especially the children who ran errands for her.

One day she noticed, to her dismay that she was

losing her hair!

Mrs Grumpold was horrified. She went to the doctor who gave her potions and pills and special shampoos, none of which stopped her hair from falling out. Every time she washed her hair, the sink looked like it was **FULL OF COBWEBS!**

Mrs Grumpold would stare in horror at the tangled mass of hair swirling around the plughole. She even thought of gluing it back in place!

Some of the more **horrid** children in the neighbourhood began to laugh at her and call her 'Baldie' or 'Egg-head'.

Mrs Grumpold was mortified. She began to stay at home even more and did not leave her house for fear of people laughing at her. Her best friend, Mabel Trotter, went shopping for her so that she did not have to leave the house and walk around in public.

'What am I going to do?' she asked miserably one day. 'I'm losing my beautiful hair!'

Mabel answered immediately, 'I was wondering when you would get around to asking me about your hair,' she said. 'It's simple. Get a wig! That's what I would do if I were you.'

'A wig?'

'Yes, a wig. Cover up your head and no one will be the wiser.'

Mrs Grumpold stared at her friend in disbelief. 'W-w-where do you get wigs from, Mabel?'

'Ava, get your coat on,' Mabel answered. 'I'm taking you right now to get a wig. Come on. Let's go!'

That was it. Wearing a hat to cover her balding

head, and firmly holding Mabel's arm, Mrs Grumpold waddled to a shop on the high street and came out wearing a wig.

A pale blue wig.

She was so proud of her new wig that she had a smile on her face all the way home. Mrs Grumpold was positively beaming. She was as happy as she had been for years.

Two days later, a new family moved into the house next door.

A lovely family with five children.

Two of the children were leaning on the fence next day when Mrs Grumpold came out to hang some washing on the line. She was wearing her new wig.

'Hello, boys,' she said, a little breathlessly.

'Hello, lady,' said the biggest boy. 'What's your name?'

Before she could answer the other boy laughed.

'You've got blue hair!' he said, pointing and holding his hand over his mouth.

Mrs Grumpold was very pleased because they had not spotted that this was a wig. She beamed. There were no shouts of 'Baldie' or 'Egg-head' so this was a very pleasant change.

Thank you, Mabel, she thought. *It's working already.*

'My name is Mrs Grumpold,' she said, smiling.

'Why have you got blue hair?' the boy persisted.

'Have you come to live next door to me?' she asked, ignoring the question.

'I've never seen *blue* hair before!'

'I like my hair *blue*,' said Mrs Grumpold. 'It's different to everybody else and I like to be different.' Mrs Grumpold was beginning to feel much more confident.

'We've just moved in,' said the older boy. 'My name is Orlando and this is Sylvester. He's my brother.'

'Our dad is in the SAS. He shoots people,' Sylvester announced importantly.

'We don't know that, Sylvester,' Orlando reproved. 'But he is in the SAS, Mrs Grumpold. The trouble is, we never see him,' he added sadly.

'Oh dear!' she sighed.

'He sends us letters when he gets the chance and asks us to help Ma, and look after each other 'till he comes home.'

'Oh dear,' she repeated. 'When will he come home?'

'We don't know. We only know that his work is **TOP SECRET**.'

'Gosh, that sounds very important doesn't it? A bit like James Bond,' Mrs Grumpold said looking very impressed.

'I'm going to be a cricketer when I grow up,' Sylvester added with pride. 'Just like Alastair Cook. He's the greatest. I'm going to be England captain, just like him, and score loads of runs. He is my favourite batsman.'

'Ooh, that's nice. My husband Harvey used to play cricket,' she replied.

'Was he a bowler? I want to be a batsman or wicket keeper,' Sylvester added. 'I'm good at throwing and I like batting. I scored forty-three yesterday.'

'Forty-three! Well, that's a good innings. Well

done!'

'No, not an *innings*. I scored forty-three with one hit,' Sylvester said grinning.

'Are you sure?' Mrs Grumpold asked. 'I think six is the highest score you can make with one hit.'

'Yes, I'm sure. It was forty-three.'

'It was a lost ball!' Orlando explained. 'It went down the road and got stuck under a parked car! Ma called us in for tea otherwise I think he would still be running now!'

Mrs Grumpold smiled. 'Bless!' she said. 'My Harvey was a wicket keeper and a very good batsman.'

'Did he play for England?' Sylvester asked.

'Oh dear, no!' she said. 'He played for Kings Heath Amateur Cricket Club.'

'Is that in Australia?' Sylvester queried.

'No, it's just down the road by the allotments.'

'Allotments? What are they?' Orlando asked.

'It's where some local people go to grow their own vegetables,' Mrs Grumpold answered, smiling. 'They plant seeds and they grow into all sorts of things. Harvey used to grow lovely tomatoes,' she said reminiscing.

'That doesn't sound very exciting,' Orlando replied pulling a face.

'Oh, I agree,' said Mrs Grumpold. 'It's not my cup of tea!'

'I thought you said they grow vegetables not tea,' Sylvester said looking **BAFFLED**.

'Ignore him,' Orlando said, mocking his younger brother. 'He looks intelligent, but, in his case, looks are deceiving!'

Mrs Grumpold smiled again. 'Would you like to earn 50p?' she asked them.

'Is that fifty pence each, or fifty pence between us?' Orlando asked shrewdly.

'Well, it's a lot of money so, it will be between you.'

'That's 25p each, Sylvie,' Orlando observed, waiting for Sylvester to shriek in anger.

'I *know* that! And don't call me Sylvie!' he yelled.

Orlando smiled and Mrs Grumpold looked on with wide-eyes wondering what *that* was all about.

'What do we have to do?' Orlando asked.

'Would you be little angels and pop to the shop on

the corner and get me a few candles? It's my birthday on Sunday and I haven't got any candles for my cake yet.'

'How old are you?' Sylvester butted in.

'I will be sixty-eight,' she said beaming.

'That's *very* old!' Sylvester shrieked.

How many candles would you like?' Orlando asked.

'Well, I have thought about that carefully and—'

SYLVESTER CUT HER OFF. 'You will *never* get sixty-eight candles on one cake unless it's as big as the table!'

Mrs Grumpold smiled.

Orlando winced. 'I think he's right, Mrs Grumpold,' he said.

'Yes, I know,' she replied. 'I was going to say that I need fourteen candles.'

'*Fourteen*!' Sylvester hooted. 'That won't be anywhere near enough!'

Mrs Grumpold smiled at him wisely and patiently. 'Oh, but it will,' she insisted. 'Fourteen is perfect.'

Orlando studied her closely. 'I think you've got a plan in mind,' he said trying to make her feel a little more comfortable. *Sylvester needs to learn a bit more tact,* he thought to himself.

'Yes I have,' she said.

'Can I see if I can work it out?' Orlando asked. 'Is it one candle for every seven years?'

'No,' she replied.

'Aah no, of course not,' Orlando said. 'That would mean you are ninety-eight! Seven times fourteen is ninety-eight.'

'I hope I don't look that old,' Mrs Grumpold said, grinning.

'And it's not one for every five years because that would mean you are seventy.'

'Right again,' she responded. 'Do you want to give up?'

'Not yet,' Orlando replied, deep in thought. 'You're sixty-eight... so that gives eight candles for the last eight years.'

'Well done! So where do the other six candles come from?' she prompted.

'I've got it!' Orlando said with a SNAP of his fingers. 'One for every ten years. Am I right?'

'You *are* right,' she said. 'That's very clever! Now, would you go and get me fourteen candles for my cake from the shop?'

'We've got nothing else to do,' Orlando replied, smiling.

'Are you having a party?' Sylvester asked.

'Yes, of course! Doesn't everybody have a party for their birthday? Even if they are sixty-eight.'

Orlando laughed and **CLAPPED** his hands. 'I think that's a great idea. When is your party and can we come to it?'

'Well, since you're my new neighbours, it would be my pleasure er, erm – what was your name again?' she asked.

'It's Orlando and this is Sylvester, my brother.'

'OK,' she said with a smile. 'You're invited. It is on Sunday afternoon. Now, if you come around to the front door, I will have the money for you for the candles. I've just got to go in and find my purse.'

Two minutes later, the boys were knocking on Mrs Grumpold's front door. She gave them a two-pound coin and they began to walk to the shop. 'You can spend fifty pence on yourselves.' She called. 'And I want the change.'

'Of course!' Orlando called back.

'OK, Mrs Grumpy,' Sylvester muttered under his breath. Orlando laughed.

On Sunday afternoon, the whole family was sitting in Mrs Grumpold's front room with **LOTS** of other people helping Ava Grumpold to **celebrate** her birthday.

There were sandwiches and cakes, sausage rolls and jelly laid out on a table in her other room and, when everyone was sitting down eating, Mrs Grumpold made the announcement. 'Well, it's time to light the candles on my cake.'

'Please can *I* light them,' Orlando asked putting his hand up.

Mrs Grumpold hesitated.

'I've done it before,' Orlando quickly added, when he noticed her reluctance.

He looked so keen that Mrs Grumpold gave in. 'All right,' she said, 'but please be very careful. We don't want you to burn yourself.'

She gave him a long plastic lighter about 20cm long. Orlando stared at it. It looked a bit like a gun.

It had a trigger.

'Squeeze the trigger,' Ma said.

He did, and a small flame shot out of the end. Orlando smiled and repeated the action several times.

'Don't wear it out,' said Ma. 'Just light the candles.'

Orlando leaned forward over the cake. There were fourteen candles making a circle around the edge and pink icing writing in the middle saying

HAPPY BIRTHDAY
AVA.

Orlando began to light the fourteen candles.

'Light the ones at the back first,' said Mrs Grumpold, 'so you don't burn your hand when you reach over.'

One of the candles was difficult to light and

Orlando had to try several times before it fired up. He was enjoying himself. *This firelighter is brilliant!* he thought.

When the last of the candles was lit, Mabel took charge. 'OK, everybody, let's sing.' She began...

'Happy Birthday to you,''

...and they all joined in.

Unfortunately, the troublesome candle went out again near the end of the song, just as Mrs Grumpold was about to blow them all out.

'Make a wish as you blow them out!' Mabel called to Mrs Grumpold. **EVERYONE CLAPPED.**

'Yes – make a wish,' some of her friends called out.

'No! Just a minute,' Orlando shouted. 'One of the candles has gone out. I will have to relight it,' and he leaned over, **clicking** the lighter switch, just as Mrs Grumpold leaned over to blow.

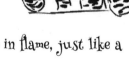

The next second, her wig went up in flame, just like a bonfire!

'*Aah*!' she squealed. 'Oh my goodness, I'm on fire!'

SEVERAL OF THE LADIES SCREAMED.

Mabel ran into the kitchen for a tea towel and held it under the tap to wet it, but Sylvester was the first to react.

He was still holding his glass of squash and quickly threw it over the flaming wig. It was a great throw and most of the flames were extinguished.

BUT NOT ALL.

Mrs Grumpold gasped as the cold drink took her breath away and an ice cube slithered its way down the front of her dress!

As she was trying to grab the **SLIPPERY** ice cube, Mabel appeared with the dripping wet tea towel and threw it over the wretched Mrs Grumpold. The wig and her entire head disappeared under the towel and cold water dripped down her neck. Mrs Grumpold squealed again.

'Get it off me! Get it off me!'

Mabel dragged it off and the wig moved with it! It was now blue and black, and steam was rising from it.

They all stared. Mrs Grumpold's wig sat halfway across her face and leaned over at an angle. Then, slowly, it teetered and –

Fell to the floor!

There were gasps from all around the room and everyone stared at Mrs Grumpold's bald head! This was a birthday she would never forget!

CHAPTER TWO
Summertime Blues

Orlando and Sylvester were exploring their new neighbourhood. They were carrying wooden sticks like guns, commando-style over their arms – just like their dad, who was somewhere in the world saving lives and sorting out terrorists.

'Can't see any hostiles over here,' Sylvester muttered.

'Copy that,' Orlando replied. 'That's a negative.' They both looked around **INTENTLY** and, suddenly, a car pulled up next to them. The boys stepped back to look at the car, then aimed their stick guns at the man inside.

The driver, Cedric Gamboll, saw them straight away and immediately held his hands up. 'Don't shoot soldiers!' he called. 'I'm unarmed and extremely un-dangerous!' He grinned at them.

Orlando realised the man was having some fun and **grinned** back. In his best American accent, he said, 'Get out of the car slowly and keep your hands where I can see them or you'll get filled with lead, you dirty rat!'

Cedric climbed out of the car and walked around to the pavement with both hands held high. He was a short, slim man who looked to be in his eighties.

'Are you a gangster?' Sylvester asked.

'No, I've just been to the DIY store to get some paint. I'm going to decorate my lounge,' Cedric replied, laughing. 'Are you two gangsters?'

'No, we're commandos,' Orlando answered. 'Just like our dad. He's in the SAS.'

'Is he now?' Mr Gamboll responded. 'That sounds very exciting. Please can I put my hands down?'

The boys looked at each other questioningly. 'Seems OK to me,' said Orlando, nodding.

'Me too,' Sylvester agreed. 'OK, mister. You can lower your hands now, *but don't try anything tricky!*'

'Oh, I wouldn't dream of it,' Mr Gamboll responded. 'Now, who are you two and where are you commandos going?'

'I'm Sylvester and he is Orlando. We're scouting the area for hostiles,' Sylvester informed him.

'Hostiles, eh? I've lived here for twenty-two years and the only hostile I have ever seen was my wife with a rolling pin in her hand. I thought she was going to throw it at me!'

Orlando laughed.

'I've never seen you lads before. Where are you from?' Mr Gamboll continued his questioning.

'We moved in next door to Mrs Grumpold a few days ago,' Orlando told him.

'Aah, yes. She mentioned it to me the day after her birthday party. You're **THOSE KIDS NEXT DOOR**, aren't you?'

Orlando nodded, remembering the wig incident. 'Where is your paint?' Orlando asked, quickly changing the subject. 'Can we help you to carry it? We like to help people.'

'Especially old people, like you and Mrs Grumpy,'

Sylvester butted in.

Orlando **GLARED** at him wide-eyed and open-mouthed. Mr Gamboll laughed.

'You are very kind, but I don't need any help, thank you. I can manage. It's only a small tin,' he said. 'Is it OK if I go around the car and get it out of the boot? I don't want you to think I'm getting a machine gun out!'

They all **laughed** and the boys watched as Cedric Gamboll opened the car boot. There were several shopping bags. He lifted the tin of paint out first and placed it on the pavement, then reached back in to gather some of the shopping bags.

'What colour is the paint?' Sylvester enquired.

'It's blue. I like blue,' he replied, setting some of the bags down by the paint tin. He lifted out the remaining bags with one hand and closed the boot with the other. Cedric Gamboll turned to pick up the shopping on the pavement but, before he could do so, Sylvester had grabbed the handle of the tin of paint in both hands. He lifted it with a struggle.

'Ugh,' he grunted with the strain.

'That's too heavy for you, Sylvie,' Orlando

mocked. 'Give it to me to carry.' Orlando reached to take the paint from his younger brother and immediately regretted calling him 'Sylvie.'

SYLVESTER HAD THE LOOK OF ANGER IN HIS EYES. 'My name is *Sylvester*!' he yelled and yanked the tin of paint from Orlando's grasp.

'Boys, please take care!' Cedric called out. He looked extremely worried. 'Please put the tin down. I'll carry it.' But it was too late.

Orlando now had both hands on the handle and was having a tug of war with Sylvester. '*I* will carry the paint,' he blurted through his teeth. '*Let go!*'

'No! I won't let go!' Sylvester yelled back. '*I'm* going to carry it!'

'But it's too heavy for you.'

'*No, it's not!*'

'You can hardly lift it – look! You're struggling.'

All this time the tin of paint was **lurching** one way, then the other and Mr Gamboll looked on, horrified. He knew what was about to happen and could do *nothing* to stop it.

'No, I'm *not*!'

'Yes you –' Orlando did not finish. As he yanked hard, the plastic handle broke and the paint tin flew up past his head, rolling over and over, to land with a dull 'crunch' on its rim on the pavement where it **BURST** open spilling beautiful blue paint.

The paint spattered up the car and spread over the pavement. It was on Mr Gamboll's feet and on the shopping bags too.

Sylvester and Orlando leapt backwards away from it.

'Oh dear!' was all Cedric Gamboll could say. 'Oh dear!' He stood still. SHAKING. He shook from head to toe.

'I guess this means we don't get fifty pence!' Sylvester whined.

'Quick,' said Orlando. 'Get something to clean it up with!' He looked around and remembered Mrs Grumpold's washing line. 'Go and see if Mrs Grumpold has got any tea towels on her washing line.'

Sylvester disappeared into her back garden and returned carrying several tea towels. The boys began to mop up the paint with the towels while Mr Gamboll stood quite still saying, 'Oh dear! Oh dear!' He had not moved from the spot.

Orlando tried to wipe the paint from the silver car and the rear wing became blue. He wiped the shopping bags that Mr Gamboll was holding and they became blue. He wiped the paint on his shoes and they became blue. He wiped Mr Gamboll's trouser legs. There was blue everywhere. It was like a sea of blue.

Mrs Grumpold looked out of her window and immediately rang **999.**

On the other side of the road, several people stopped to watch the drama and quite a crowd gathered, chatting, frowning and laughing.

One lady crossed the road and gently led Mr

Gamboll away from the paint. He was still whimpering, 'Oh dear, oh dear,' quietly and left a trail of blue footprints. They stopped and stood on his front lawn watching the two boys trying to clean up, but making everything worse. Paint dripped from the bags that he was still holding. 'Oh dear!' he whispered. 'Oh dear!'

Suddenly, the siren of a fire engine was heard in the distance, getting closer. Within seconds, it **SQUEALED** to a halt and four firefighters leapt out carrying various pieces of equipment. The lady firefighter threw a drain mat over the drain by the kerb to stop the paint from going down into the drains and her colleague began to spread crystals over the paint. Another carried a bucket of sand and the last firefighter carried a foam cylinder.

Mrs Grumpold came out to get a better view and was standing in her hot pink slippers at the end of her path.

Sylvester felt **GUILTY** and took the tea towel that he was holding over to her. He held it out but she declined saying, 'Sylvester, haven't you lads done enough damage to me already?'

Blue paint dripped onto her slippers. She looked down at them and she wailed **LOUDLY.**

'Oh, I'm so sorry, Mrs Grumpy,' he said apologetically and began to wipe the paint off the slippers with the paint-covered tea towel! There was now paint on her ankles. Mrs Grumpold shrieked and jumped back. She kicked off both slippers and ran back inside her house.

Later that evening, two police officers called to the house of **THOSE KIDS NEXT DOOR** to have a long chat with their mother.

CHAPTER THREE
Eggstrordinary
Pigeons

'I'm fed up with those pigeons, Ava,' Florence Mildew declared. She was leaning on the fence talking to Mrs Grumpold. They had been neighbours and friends for thirty-two years. 'They have recently started to sit on my bedroom windowsill above my front door.'

She pushed her scarf up.

UNDERNEATH THE SCARF, SHE HAD LOADS OF HAIR CURLERS.

Ava could not remember a time when Florence did *not* wear those curlers. It was as if she was always getting ready for some important date and had to have her hair looking marvellous. But she never went anywhere important!

'They keep pooing and it drops down on the floor outside my front door.' She pushed her scarf up once more. 'I slipped in that poo yesterday and nearly fell over and did myself a nasty,' she said indignantly. 'There are six pigeons all in a line. I don't know why they sit there all day pooing.'

Orlando and Sylvester Shufflett were on the other side of the fence with their brother Tyrone, and sister Channing. They were playing cricket. Channing loved cricket but Sylvester was the best batsman. Orlando overheard the conversation and **HISSED** at his brothers and sister. 'Shh! Listen. She is talking about somebody pooing!'

They all laughed and sat down by the fence listening.

'Are you feeding them, Flo?' Mrs Grumpold asked. 'Because that will encourage them. You know that.'

'Of course I'm not feeding them. Do I look *that* stupid?' she said crossly, pushing up her scarf again.

Ava Grumpold studied her friend thinking, *Yes, you* do *look that stupid!* but decided not to say it.

'Well they must have a reason for sitting there.

They are not having choir practice are they?' she said laughing.

'It's not a laughing matter, Ava. They could poo on me when I go out!'

The three boys giggled. 'The poo would get stuck in her curlers,' Orlando blurted and little Tyrone thought it was *very* funny.

'I'm frightened in case I leave the house and they all poo *together*!' This made both of the ladies laugh and the Shufflett children were now hysterical.

'They sit facing the road, then, when they want a poo, they turn around and dangle their bums over the edge and down it plops! On *my* path!' Florence looked dismayed and did not know whether to laugh or cry.

Ava HOOTED like an owl and was laughing wildly now and, in the next door garden, Orlando was having a great time. 'Plopping poos,' he said. 'They are poo plopping pigeons having a proper poo plopping festival.' They all laughed loudly.

'It's a Poo Fest,' said Sylvester and they all joined in. 'Poo Fest, Poo Fest.'

'What am I going to do, Ava?' Florence asked

looking exasperated.

'Have you tried opening your window and scaring them away?'

'Yes, and they keep coming back.'

Orlando whispered loudly behind his hand, 'She's only got to stand near the window and stare at them to scare them!' He pulled a face and they laughed. 'She would make a good scarecrow!'

'Do you think I should ring the council and see if they can do anything about them, Ava?' Mrs Mildew asked despairingly.

'Well, it's either that or put your umbrella up every time you leave the house!' Ava suggested with another giggle.

Ma called them in for lunch and RELUCTANTLY they went in.

Afterwards, Orlando and Sylvester went for a walk to the park. As they went past Mrs Mildew's house, she appeared on the doorstep, nervously looking upwards. 'Hey, lads, would you be kind and go to the shop for me and I'll give you fifty pence?' she called.

'Yes,' they answered together. 'What do you want?'

'I need some eggs and a loaf of bread.'

They walked down the path to the front door staring up at the windowsill, hoping not to get POOED on. The six pigeons sat looking down at them. Carefully, Orlando took the money and a bag from Mrs Mildew and they ran back up the path just in time to miss **TWO PLOPS!**

*

On the way back from the shop, they began talking about the pigeons. 'Why don't we scare them off for her?' Orlando suggested. 'It's a real shame. She is so fed up with them.'

'That's a good idea, but *how*?' Sylvester queried.

'I'm not sure. Maybe we could make loud noises.'

'Or use a stick to knock them off,' Sylvester offered.

'It would need to be a very long stick!' Orlando pointed out.

They arrived back at Mrs Mildew's house and stood halfway down the path, looking up at the pigeons. The pigeons stared back at them.

'Why don't we throw stones at them?' Sylvester said, and picked up a whopper from the garden.

'No, don't be silly! You might break the window if you miss!'

'I won't miss. I'm a good thrower.'

'OK, so you will *injure* the pigeon. That's *not* a good idea, Sylvester. We need something soft that will scare them, but won't hurt them or break the window.' He began to look around for something suitable.

Sylvester had the answer and was beginning to

open the box of eggs, **GRINNING.**

Orlando turned and saw what he was doing. 'Great idea!' he shouted and Sylvester launched the first egg.

It **SPLATTED** harmlessly on the wall by the side of the sill and the pigeons looked down at them smugly.

'Bad luck, Sylvie,' he murmured, knowing that would wind him up.

'*Sylvester!*' yelled Sylvester LAUNCHING the second egg. It soared between two pigeons and smashed against the window. One pigeon turned around and dropped a plop as if to say 'is that your best shot?'

Orlando encouraged him to greater accuracy. 'Go on, you can do this,' he said.

Sylvester gave the next egg his full concentration taking deliberate aim. But it **smashed** against the sill that the pigeons were sitting on. 'Aargh!' he screamed in frustration, 'missed again!'

He threw two more eggs, but they both crashed against the window and drizzled down as a gooey mess! 'Aargh!' he screamed again in frustration.

He carefully picked up the last egg, calmed himself and took a deep breath.

'*This time, I'll get you!*' he yelled in anger and hurled the egg at the two pigeons in the middle. It hit one of the pigeons full on the chest and shattered. They all flapped up and away into the sky. Sylvester made a high fist and pulled it down to his chin powerfully.

'Yes-s-s-s-s!'

'Great shot, Sylvester!' Orlando yelled and slapped him on the back.

There were no pigeons on the windowsill now, so they knocked the door confidently, and Mrs Mildew opened it anxiously, looking upwards.

'Don't worry, Mrs Mildew, we got rid of the pigeons for you. They won't poo on you again,' Orlando said jubilantly.

'How do you know? she asked. 'What did you do?'

'Come out and have a look,' Orlando announced proudly. 'They are *gone*.' He beckoned for her to come out.

'It's OK. It's safe now,' he said reassuringly.

Slowly and hesitantly Florence Mildew came out

of her front door and looked up to see that all the pigeons were, in fact, gone. A nervy smile began to appear on her face, but when she saw the mess all over her window, and the wall, and the windowsill she put her hand to her mouth. 'What have you done with my eggs?!' she exclaimed.

The boys looked at each other, dropped the bag with the bread and ran.

Later that day, Mrs Mildew called at the house of **THOSE KIDS NEXT DOOR** to have a word with the children's mother.

CHAPTER FOUR
Someone's Knocking
at the Door

They weren't looking for trouble; just a bit of fun, but it had to be dark. **THIS WAS PERFECT.**

The two boys ambled silently past a row of terraced houses, furtively looking around, checking for anyone who might spoil their bit of fun.

There were eight houses joined together, side by side, in a neat straight row and, between each pair of houses, there was an alley leading through to the back gardens. On either side of the alley was the front door to each house.

In front of **EVERY** house was a long, lawned garden ending with a privet hedge – a shared path led from the privet hedge to the alley.

The boys stood by the privet hedge looking down the path to the two front doors next to Mr Gamboll's house.

These were the houses where Ada Turnock and Harry Glimp lived, side by side.

'Let's do Ada's house first,' said Orlando. He was wearing a camouflage jacket and carried a large reel of twine that he had found in a cupboard of their new house. *This might come in useful one day,* he had thought at the time.

'Is it that one?' asked Sylvester, pointing to the house on the right of the alley.

'Yes, come on,' replied Orlando, and, crouching down, they SCAMPERED, COMMANDO-STYLE, up the path towards the door.

They sat, dead still, listening and catching their breath. *'Careful, Sylvester!'* whispered Orlando. 'Keep away from the window. They've got a light on.'

'I *am* being careful, Orlando!' he hissed back with irritation.

Orlando ignored him and gently opened the

letterbox, listening for any sounds from inside the house. He could hear the faint sound of a television and a lady laughing.

'She's watching the telly,' he said. 'You look out for anyone coming while I tie the twine to the door knocker.'

Orlando lifted the door knocker and held it up firmly. It was a hinged metal handle which you **BANGED** down onto a metal plate.

'Careful, Orlando!' warned Sylvester, smirking, mimicking his older brother.

Orlando looked at him scornfully and tutted. *'Belt up!'* he hissed.

Sylvester grinned at his older brother.

Orlando began to tie the end of the twine to the door knocker. He tied several knots, to make sure that the twine would not slip off.

'That will do it nicely, Sylvester,' he murmured as he gave it a gentle tug to test it. 'Now, you hold this handle and don't let it bang down while I unroll the twine all the way down the path.'

Sylvester knew exactly what to do. They had

practised this on their own door knocker earlier that day.

Sylvester looked around. 'You're OK,' he said. 'There's no one coming.'

Slowly, Orlando edged backwards down the path, toward the privet hedge, unwinding the reel, while Sylvester continued to hold the door knocker.

They did not want any mistakes at this stage.

Orlando arrived at the privet hedge and crouched down behind it, out of sight from the house and his brother. Sylvester could not see him now so, Orlando whispered '*OK*,' just loud enough for Sylvester to hear him.

'Lower it gently and come here.'

Carefully Sylvester lowered the door knocker without a sound until it rested on the metal plate. He then swiftly tip-toed towards Orlando, crouching behind the hedge, and watched as his brother cut the twine by scraping it against the corner of the concrete fence post until it split.

THEY GRINNED AT EACH OTHER. THIS WAS GETTING EXCITING.

Orlando left the end of the twine looped around a privet branch. **ADA'S HOUSE WAS NOW READY FOR THE FUN.**

They checked up and down the road then crept back up the path and repeated the process on the Harry's door knocker.

Both houses now had twine tied to their door knockers. The twine went all the way down the path to the privet hedge behind which the two boys were now crouching, **GIGGLING** and holding one end each.

Orlando held the twine to Ada's door knocker and Sylvester was holding the end attached to Harry's door.

The hard work was done and now it was time for some fun!

'Are you ready for this, Sylvester?' Orlando said grinning.

'I sure am! Let's do it!' he replied.

Orlando gently pulled the twine towards him, gradually taking up the slack until he felt the resistance of the knocker – just as they had practised this morning. The door knocker now hovered,

menacingly, over the metal plate. CAUTIOUSLY Orlando looked up and down the street. There was no one in sight. Quickly he released the twine and giggled as the door knocker **HAMMERED** down.

Bang!

It took quite some time before the door swung open and a large lady looked out. She peered both ways then went back inside.

Sylvester gave a nervous laugh. Orlando turned to look at him and they both grinned. 'You OK?' Orlando asked.

'Yeah, sure,' Sylvester replied, a little nervously.

'Stop worrying. It'll be all right,' Orlando said reassuringly and he took up the slack and let the knocker bang down once more.

Bang!

The lady reappeared. 'Who's that?' she called out.

Behind the hedge, the two boys giggled hysterically.

Ada stepped outside for a better look. 'Who's there? Is anyone there?'

'Yes, we are,' Orlando whispered and they both

giggled.

Ada turned and went back inside.

'Your turn,' Orlando said. Sylvester smiled, his apprehension fading away as he quickly took up the slack in his twine and '**KNOCKED'** Harry's door.

Bang!

A tall man with a beard opened the door. He looked about then went inside. The boys held their hands to their mouths to stifle their laughter.

Sylvester '**KNOCKED'** again.

Bang!

Harry opened the door again, stepped outside and looked around. He scratched his head and went back inside, muttering, 'Could've sworn I heard that door knocker.'

'My turn,' said Orlando, and he 'knocked' Ada's door.

Bang!

Ada re-emerged, looking quite angry, '*If I get my hands on you, you'll be very sorry!*' she shouted as she **SLAMMED** the door closed.

'Now you,' Orlando said to Sylvester. Sylvester

knocked Harry's door again.

Bang!

Harry stepped out, looked down the dark alley then, before going back inside, he shouted 'Pack it in – **NOW!**' then went inside and closed his door.

The two boys sat giggling until a large man came around the corner heading towards them. He seemed to be wearing a uniform and looked at the boys suspiciously. It was a policeman!

The two boys stood up with the twine hidden behind their backs.

They watched nervously as he got closer.

He seemed to be staring at them. Glaring at them.

''Allo, 'allo, 'allo. Shouldn't you boys be at home at this time of night?' he asked. Before they could say anything, he continued, 'Where do you live?'

'Er... we live just there a few doors away,' Orlando said, pointing. 'We've been to the shop for our Ma.'

'Right, well you had better get moving then,' he retorted. 'Go on! Get in before you catch cold.'

'Erm, we will when we, I mean, erm . . . yes, we are just going but. . . *he* dropped the 50p change and we were just looking for it. It rolled under this hedge,' Orlando blurted.

'Oh I see,' said the policeman. 'Well, hurry up and find it. I don't want to see you two here when I come back in half an hour.'

'Oh no, sir. It shouldn't take long to find it.' The boys both bent down and **pretended** to be searching.

The policeman said, 'Good night, boys,' and walked away. *Hurry up now,'* he called.

'Good night, policeman,' they called back and watched him until he disappeared down the road.

They looked at each other and breathed a sigh of relief.

'Oh my giddy aunt,' said Sylvester. 'I'm not doing this anymore. I don't want to get into trouble!'

'Phew!' said Orlando.

'Come on. Let's go home now.' Sylvester whimpered.

'Don't be a scaredy-cat. Come on, one more time,' Orlando encouraged him.

Sylvester looked for the policeman, then, seeing no one about, reluctantly picked up the end of the twine ready to restart the action.

'OK. Now let's knock together and get them to come outside at the *same* time,' Orlando muttered. 'OK?'

Sylvester nodded. They pulled in the slack and, when they were both ready, Orlando said, 'After three. Ready? One, two, *three*!' They both released the twine at the same time and the two door knockers banged down simultaneously.

Bang!

BOTH DOORS SWUNG OPEN.

'Pack it up now!' shouted the lady at the same time as Harry leapt out through his door. He turned and spotted her. He did not look happy and pointed an angry finger at her.

'Are you knocking my door, Ada?'

'NO!' she scowled. 'Why would I do that Harry? I reckon it's **THOSE KIDS NEXT DOOR** to Mrs Grumpold!' She turned to look down the path to the road and yelled, 'Right, I've had enough. Clear off!' The boys **SQUIRTED** their laughs out through their hands, trying hard not to be heard.

The adults held a quiet conversation behind their hands then went inside.

The boys knocked again and, this time they tugged and released *repeatedly*, rapping the knockers over and over again.

Bang!

Bang! Bang!

Bang! Bang! Bang!

Suddenly both doors swung open – ripping the twine out of their hands – and two very angry adults stepped outside.

The adults stood glaring about them, ready for action, then they charged down the path towards the two boys.

'*We'd better move, fast!*' yelled Orlando and stood up, hauling his younger brother to his feet at the same time.

'I knew it was you two!' Ada snarled, leading the way down the path. 'Come on, Harry, let's get them!'

The boys ran across the gardens, and disappeared down the black hole that was the entry to their back yard. They flew in through the gate and Orlando **SNAPPED** the shoot bolt to lock it. They leaned their backs against it as if making sure that no one was going to get through this gate.

Ada and Harry did not try to follow them. Instead, they knocked at the front door and had a long chat with their mother.

Ma was waiting for the two boys when they sneaked in through the back door.

She was angry!

VERY ANGRY!

CHAPTER FIVE
Run and Get the Fire Brigade

Bernard Wegley LOVED his shed. He spent hours in it making all sorts of things like paper aeroplanes, balsa wood aeroplanes, toy tanks that moved, origami models, candle holders, egg cups, table mats, coat hangers and coasters. He would go down to his shed at the bottom of his garden when it got light and went back to the house when it got dark. **THERE WAS NO ELECTRICITY IN BERNARD'S SHED.**

Bernard lived on his own with Herbie, his dog, and Nemo, his goldfish. His wife had left him many years before saying, *'What's the point of living together when we don't see each other? You're always in **that** shed!'* She left him and went to live in Greece where it was warmer and there were no sheds.

It was a month before Bernard realised she had gone!

'Ah well,' he told himself, 'that's one less thing to worry about.' Bernard was unflappable.

Herbie was a very old dog and spent most of the time asleep, curled up in his bed by the side of the television. Next to Herbie was the goldfish bowl which stood on the hearth by the fireplace. In the bowl, there was a miniature castle and some pretend plants. Swimming around them was Nemo, the goldfish who never seemed to sleep at all.

Mr Wegley was very often *so* busy that he forgot to sleep and **FORGOT TO GO SHOPPING**, which is why he would often have **no food** in his cupboards.

So, Bernard was ECSTATIC when the new family moved in three doors away because, for 50p, they would do his shopping for him! The two boys loved shopping for Mr Wegley and were always ready when he called to them. Sometimes the girl, Channing, did the shopping and Bernard suspected that she kept the 50p all to herself.

'What would you like today, Mr Wegley?' Orlando **SHOUTED** over the back gardens. Bernard could hear them in his shed and would normally shout back a few items or quickly write a little list and wrap the money in it. He would then place it in a bag on the front door step for the children to collect.

After shopping, the children would leave the groceries on the same step.

This worked well for a time but, one day, the food from the day before was **still there!** Mr Wegley was so busy that he had forgotten to bring it in the house. So Orlando decided to climb over the fence into Mrs Grumpold's garden then into Mrs Mildew's garden then into Mr Wegley's garden and take the items directly to his shed.

Unfortunately, Mrs Grumpold and Mrs Mildew did not like this. 'Hey you, Orlando! Sylvester! *Clear off!* Don't you go coming here in our back gardens,' they shouted.

That's when the boys learned to become DEVIOUS. They had to wait until the ladies were not looking, or had popped out to a neighbour, or were watching the telly, before they could nip over their fences to Mr Wegley's shed.

'This is exciting,' Orlando said one time. *'Just like being in the SAS for real!'*

Two days later, Mr Wegley left the bag with a list and some money as usual on the step. Orlando studied the list which read:

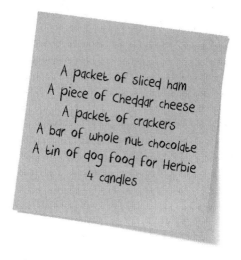

A packet of sliced ham
A piece of Cheddar cheese
A packet of crackers
A bar of whole nut chocolate
A tin of dog food for Herbie
4 candles

It was a lovely sunny day as they walked back from the shop. 'I know,' said Sylvester, 'let's go through the Park and have a quick go on the swings.'

'I don't know,' Orlando replied, hesitating. 'Mr Wegley might be waiting for these for his lunch. We should go straight back.'

'Oh, come on, Orly. Don't be a pussy cat. One quick go and then back to Mr Wegley's house. OK? It will be fun. He won't even notice the time.'

Normally, Orlando would have leapt on Sylvester and **THUMPED** him for calling him '*Orly*' but he was holding the bag of food and decided to take no notice.

'I'm not sure,' he protested.

'Five minutes. Just *five* minutes, that's all!' Sylvester persisted.

Orlando took a deep breath. 'OK, five minutes and *that's all!*'

They went into the park and ran over to the swings and Orlando carefully placed the shopping bag down by the pole. They sat on the swings and away they went. Up, up and away! **As high as they could go.**

'I'm getting better at this,' Sylvester called. 'Look I am nearly as high as you now.'

Orlando watched as six youths came into the Park. They looked to be about fourteen and were all bigger than him. He looked on, anxiously, as they headed over to the swings. There were six swings.

'I think we should get going now, Sylvester. We have had five minutes.'

'No way!' Sylvester argued.

Orlando tried to slow down as quickly as he could, but the boys arrived before he could get off. He studied them carefully and did not like what he saw.

Four of the boys sat on the remaining swings and the other two stood facing Orlando.

'Clear off, you two worms,' yelled the boy with a spotty face. 'These are *our* swings!'

'Yeah,' screamed his mate. 'And we don't like anybody else using them, so get lost!'

Orlando Smoothly slid off the swing and went to collect the shopping bag but the pimple face was already picking it up. 'Hey, Jason, he was going to take your bag. We don't like people taking our bags do we lads?'

They all laughed. 'No,' they called.

'What's in the bag, Daz?'

'Well, let's have a look.' Daz reached in and brought out the packet of ham. 'Ham!' he called and gave it to Jason by his side. He reached in again and brought out the chocolate. 'Ooh, chocolate!' he drooled and threw it to one of the boys on a swing.

'Yum, yum, Daz,' he said rubbing his stomach. 'This is going to be tasty!'

'Now what else is in the bag?' Daz called out like a TV presenter and reached in once more. 'Cheese!' he yelled. 'Stinky Cheese!'

'Please, Daz,' said Orlando. 'That food is for Mr Wegley. It's not ours.'

It's not ours,' Daz mimicked. *'It's for Mister Wegley!'*

They all laughed and copied him, *'It's for Mister Wegley!'*

'Never heard of him!' said Daz. 'So that means it's our stuff.'

Two minutes later the youths were MUNCHING all the food and Sylvester was in tears.

'Oh look, he's crying,' Jason scoffed and took the bag from Daz. 'I don't like to see boys crying,' he jeered and tipped the tin of dog food and the four candles onto the floor. He then placed the bag over Sylvester's head and laughed. 'I can't see him crying now!' They all laughed and began to walk away.

Sylvester **HEAVED** the bag off his head angrily and the brothers stood watching the six youths leaving the park.

'Do not say anything!' Orlando muttered through his teeth.

'One day I will be as big as them and they won't put a bag over my head then!' Sylvester said defiantly.

When the youths had disappeared, Orlando picked up the dog food and candles and placed them in the bag. 'Do you still think it was a fun idea to come to the park?' he said sarcastically.

On the way back Sylvester asked, 'What are we going to tell Mr Wegley?'

'The truth. That's what Ma always tells us. We tell him the truth.'

'He won't believe us,' Sylvester continued.

'We have to try.'

When they arrived at Mr Wegley's house, the door was ajar. 'I'm in the kitchen lads, making a cup of tea. Would you like a cup?'

'No thanks,' they called together, looking at each other nervously.

'Please put the bag in the cupboard and you can take the candles down to the shed if you don't mind,' Mr Wegley called.

Gratefully, and with immense relief, Orlando placed the bag in the cupboard, out of sight and they raced outside with the candles. Mr Wegley called out, 'Take care that the two 'old grumpies' don't see you when you go over the fences!' he said, laughing. 'I'm going to drink my tea before I go back to the shed. I will only be about five minutes.'

'Bye, Mr Wegley,' they said and **JOGGED** down the garden.

It was getting dark in the shed and the boys looked around, playing with some of the Origami figures and paper aeroplanes.

'We need more light in here,' Orlando observed and gave one of the candles to Sylvester to hold. He lit it using a match, then took it off his brother. He could not put it in the usual candle holder because there was a small bit of candle left, so he stood it upright.

IT FELL OVER AND WENT OUT.

Orlando lit it again and leaned it up against a low

shelf with a bottle of water on it.

Unfortunately, he did not read the label.

It read:

'OK, let's go,' he said. 'Mr Wegley will be here in a minute or so.' They scouted for the two elderly ladies and, seeing the coast was clear, they scaled the three fences on the way back to their own garden.

Channing was playing football with Tyrone and Ma was collecting the washing from the line. Beyonsay was asleep in her buggy. It was getting dark, but the two boys joined in with the football.

After a few minutes, they heard a

sound from nearby.

They all stopped playing to look around.

Channing spotted it first. 'Look!' she shouted, 'The shed is on fire!'

Orlando and Sylvester **STARED** with mouths gaping open.

'The shed is on fire! Quick! Mr Wegley could be in there!' Orlando said fearfully. Leading the way, he leapt over the fences followed by Sylvester and looked through the window into the flaming shed.

He could not see Mr Wegley so, heaving a sigh of relief, he ran up the path to the house and raced inside to find Mr Wegley asleep on the settee. Sylvester was right behind him.

'Mr Wegley. Mr Wegley. You've got to wake up. Your shed is on fire!'

Two doors away, for the second time in three weeks, Mrs Grumpold dialled **999**.

'What!' exclaimed Mr Wegley.

'Your shed is on fire!'

'Oh my goodness gracious me!' he said LEAPING to his feet to look out through the window. 'My shed is on fire!'

'Yes, that's what I told you. What are you going to do?' Orlando asked.

'Fill the bucket with water,' Mr Wegley instructed, picking up his mop bucket. He gave it to Orlando who raced with it to the kitchen sink. **HE TURNED BOTH TAPS ON FULL.** Mr Wegley searched in his cupboards for another bucket or a large vase to fill.

There was a loud bang on the front door.

'Not now,' Mr Wegley shouted. 'I'm busy. I've got a fire in my shed!'

'We know, sir. We are the fire brigade,' a voice yelled back. 'We can't get in because your back gate is locked. We've got to come through the house. Please hurry and open the door or it will be too late!'

Mr Wegley RACED to the door and ushered the firefighters in. The first one was pulling a hose pipe behind her. She raced past Mr Wegley and met Sylvester in the lounge. He was **JUMPING** up and down shouting, 'There's a fire in the shed! There's a fire in the shed.'

'I know!' she yelled. *'Get out of my way!'*

She dodged around him holding the nozzle and

immediately bumped into Orlando who was coming out of the kitchen carrying a full, very heavy bucket of water.

CRASH!

They both crashed to the floor and the water spilled EVERYWHERE!

'I'm sorry!' Orlando yelled getting up and helping the firefighter to her feet.

'You will be if you don't get out of my way – fast!' she yelled back.

Orlando stood back and she ran outside with the hose beginning to spray. He followed her to get a good view.

The next firefighter through the door was helping by pulling the hose through the house. 'Move please!' he yelled, as Sylvester got in his way.

Sylvester dodged to his right then to his left then slipped and fell under the firefighter's feet. The man tripped and crashed to the floor on top of Sylvester who screamed, 'Aargh!'

The man banged his ribs on the settee as he went down and *he* screamed, 'Aargh!'

Then, his yellow helmet thumped into the television. The television fell off the table and hit Herbie, who had been managing to stay asleep in all the chaos. Herbie shot up knocking the goldfish bowl over on the hearth. The bowl tipped up and rolled across the carpet spilling water everywhere leaving Nemo, the goldfish, gasping for breath inside the bowl which was now lying on its side, almost empty.

A third firefighter, carrying some equipment, now came through the front door that Mr Wegley was still holding open and he rushed through to the lounge where he spotted his colleague on the floor. He helped lift him to his feet and then they both lifted Sylvester and placed him down on the settee. *'Stay there!'* they said, 'and *don't* move till we *tell* you!' Sylvester nodded.

Unseen by everyone, Dinky, Mr Dinsdale's cat, slipped through the door and followed the firefighter into the lounge. Cats are very curious creatures and Dinky had come to find out what all the fuss was about.

He immediately spotted Nemo **flapping** about in his nearly-empty bowl. This was his big chance for a nice bit of fresh fish and Dinky pounced on the bowl trying to catch Nemo by hooking him out with his paw. Fortunately, Herbie spotted him and growled, scaring him off. Dinky fled outside and raced up a tree.

Mr Wegley ran over to save Nemo and slipped on the wet carpet. HE FELL HEAD OVER HEELS AND BANGED HIS HEAD ON THE OVERTURNED TELLY AND LOST CONSCIOUSNESS.

Half an hour later, the fire was out and the shed was a smouldering mess of **BLACKENED, CHARRED, WOOD.**

Mr Wegley was being loaded into an ambulance to spend the night in hospital with a big **LUMP** on his head.

'OK, you two,' said the firefighter. 'Let's go and have a word with your parents. Where do you live?' she demanded.

'Up there next to Mrs Grumpold,' Orlando muttered ruefully.

She stared at him for a few seconds. 'Are you the kids involved with the blue paint all over the pavement the other day?' she asked incredulously.

Orlando nodded. 'But – '

'I thought so,' she said. 'You're **THOSE KIDS NEXT DOOR** to Mrs Grumpold! I need a word with your mum and dad. Come on!'

CHAPTER SIX
Cats and Catapults

'Orlando, Sylvester, Tyrone, come here quick!
There's a letter from Dad!' Channing called.

Ma sat in the front room holding Baby Beyonsay
who was asleep in her arms. She also held a letter.

The three boys leapt through the door wrestling
with each other to sit on the armchair. Orlando was
holding Sylvester back and trying to sit down at the
same time. Tyrone was smacking them both with
Teddy.

'*Shhh!*' Ma hissed. 'If you wake her up, you can
look after her! Now, be *quiet*!'

They stopped fighting and looked at Beyonsay.

Orlando put a finger to his lips. '*Shhh!*' He copied
Ma and looked sternly at his brothers, wagging his

finger.

Ma gave him *the look*. 'Watch it, Orlando! Don't push your luck,' she warned.

The boys settled themselves into the armchair, with Tyrone sitting across the laps of his two older brothers.

'This has just arrived from your dad,' she began.

'Where is he?'

'Is he in America?'

'What's he doing?'

'Is he coming home soon?'

'If you stop talking and let me read the letter, you will find out,' she mouthed at them, before reading the letter aloud.

'To my beautiful wife and amazing children.

I understand that you have been moved again by the council and I hope you are settling into your new house.

I am sorry I cannot be there to help you unpack. You will just have to get on without me.

I hope the new house is bigger than the last one they put you in.

I do not know why they keep moving you. They don't seem to understand that you need to stay longer to make friends with the new neighbours, get to know them better and get on with everybody.

I am sure that anybody would want to have lovely children like you living next door because you are so helpful and considerate.

I miss you all badly and I wish that I could be there with you but, as you know, I have very important work to do which keeps me away from home. I promise you all that one day I will come back to be with you again and we can be a proper family once more. In the meantime, I hope you are all helping your ma and not fighting each other all the time.

Orlando, you must look after your two younger brothers and help your ma with the chores. You are the eldest and I expect you to set a good example to the others.'

Orlando beamed and looked at Channing with a smirk.

'Sylvester, I expect you to help Orlando to look after Tyrone. And, Channing, I

want you to make sure that Orlando does his homework.'

That took the smirk off his face!

'Orlando, your schoolwork is very important. Don't let me down - or yourself. When I get home I shall expect to see you doing as well as Channing. That's an order!'

Ma smiled.

'Remember to look after each other and stick by each other at all times. And remember your manners. I do not want to come home and find that you have all turned into a bunch of lazy layabouts.'

'That's all there is for you lot,' said Ma. 'The rest of the letter is for me, but Dad does finish by saying,

'I love you with all of my heart and miss you all madly. Ma will give you a big hug from me. Xx'

'OK, now I want you to go and tidy the bedroom and lounge. There are toys everywhere. Go on. Hop to it.'

'After we have had our hug, Ma,' Orlando insisted.

Ma gave them each a hug, then Sylvester and Orlando **BOUNCED** out of the kitchen like rabbits and Tyrone joined in. 'Boing, boing, boing,' they called.

In the small bedroom that the three boys shared, Sylvester and Tyrone began to collect up toys to put away. Orlando sat making a paper aeroplane.

At the bottom of the stairs Ma shouted, 'Are you doing *your* share, Orlando, or have I got to come up there and *check*?'

Orlando threw the plane at Sylvester and moved a piece of Lego with his foot. 'Yes, Ma. Course I am!'

'No he isn't, Ma!' Sylvester yelled. 'He's been making a paper aeroplane!'

Orlando **SNEERED** at him. '*Pants!*' he muttered and began to pick up the pieces of a jigsaw just as Ma appeared at the door. 'See, Ma! I *am* helping,' he said.

'OK. When you have finished this room, you can go and tidy the lounge. THEN you can go out to play.' She disappeared with an armful of towels.

'This is boring,' Orlando whinged. 'Let's hurry up and we can go outside.' He quickly threw the pieces of jigsaw under the bed then scraped other toys and books with his foot until they disappeared under the bed too.

'Come on, you two. Throw *everything* under the bed!'

After finishing the lounge, the three boys played cricket in the back garden until they became bored.

'I know!' cried Sylvester. 'Let's go and have a look at those gardening things down the street.'

'What gardening things?' Orlando asked.

'You know, the ones Mrs Grumpold told us about. Where the people grow their own vegetables.'

'Oh, the *allotments.*' Orlando reminded him. *'Absolutely, very super!'* Orlando scoffed. 'Super. Spiffing, smashing! That will be great fun, I *don't* think!'

'Oh, come on, Orlando. What else is there to do? I'm bored.'

'Well, there won't be *anything* to do at the allotments. It's just a bunch of grown-ups digging. 'I'd rather drink cold cabbage juice with blood from a dead dog's eye! Let's go to the park instead and play on the swings.'

'I'm *not* going there again – *ever*! Not until Dad's

here to sort those lads out.'

'That could be a long wait then,' Orlando said disconsolately.

'Where is Daddy?' Tyrone suddenly asked.

'Tyrone, don't talk so much. You will wear your mouth out!' Orlando said, laughing. Tyrone smiled and hid his face behind his teddy. Tyrone was wearing his little backpack as usual.

'Come on, let's put teddy in your backpack and you can hold our hands and have a swing.' Orlando **SQUISHED** teddy into the backpack.

'We could take our catapults.' Sylvester persisted. 'There might be something we can practise on.'

Without waiting for a reply, he **RACED** indoors and returned carrying the catapults.

He stared hard at Orlando then, getting no response, he tried a different tactic. 'Tyrone would you like to go to the gardens? We can swing you all the way!'

Tyrone nodded and took hold of their hands. He looked up at them, smiling.

'OK, why not?' Orlando said, heaving a sigh. 'Let's put these catapults into your backpack, then we can swing you.'

They walked down the road with Tyrone in the middle holding their hands and swinging back and forth.

'Let's see if we can get you to turn right over!' Sylvester suggested. 'Jump your feet as high as you can and do a backwards gambol.'

'But **don't** let go of our hands!' Orlando added. 'I don't want to take you home with a flat head! Ma would *not* like that.'

After several unsuccessful attempts, Tyrone managed to do a complete turnover. **HE WAS DELIGHTED.** '*Again!*' he called. So they did – loads more times!

They went past the shop and finally arrived at:

RAILWAY SIDINGS

ALLOTMENTS

There was a high, green, metal railing fence all around the allotments, but the gate was open and the boys could see several grown-ups hard at work, digging, weeding and hoeing their crops. Some plants seemed to be held up by bamboo canes and were taller than the people!

'This doesn't look very exciting,' Orlando **SNEERED**, pulling a face. 'Let's go to the park.'

'I'm definitely *not* going there again. Those boys might be there,' Sylvester countered.

A man walked past them going into the allotments carrying a white bucket. 'Hello, lads, what are *you* doing here?' he asked cheerfully.

'We're bored,' Orlando replied. 'There's nothing to do around here that's *anywhere close* to exciting.'

'You can say that again,' the man said.

'OK, *there's nothing to do around here* . . .' Orlando stopped and grinned. '*Only* joking,' he said with a laugh. **THE MAN LAUGHED TOO.**

Tyrone spotted something moving inside the bucket and asked, 'What is in your bucket, Mr Man?'

A ginger cat leapt out and ran off towards the

recently completed modern club house.

'That's my cat, Dinky. He comes with me to the allotments every day. He keeps the rats away.'

'Ugh, have you got rats around here?' said Sylvester wincing.

'Unfortunately, yes we have. But Dinky chases them off.'

'I hope we don't see any,' Sylvester added.

The man smiled and changed the subject. 'Have you ever picked strawberries? Now, *that's* not boring.'

'*Picked* strawberries?' Sylvester asked wide-eyed. 'No. We always get ours from a supermarket in a plastic container. Where can we *pick* them?'

'Well, you can't at the moment, because they are not ready but you can pick them here in my allotment when they are ripe.'

'When will they be ripe?' Orlando asked.

'Not until June,' the man answered pulling a funny face at Tyrone.

Tyrone laughed. 'You're funny!' he said.

'June!' yelled Orlando. 'I will be dead by then. I need food *every day*.' They all laughed.

'I tell you what *is* ready to pick. My *sprouts*. They're ready. Would you like to help me pick some? I promise it will only be a *little bit* boring!' The man smiled at them.

'I can't eat sprouts,' Orlando announced. 'They give me the *farts*.'

Sylvester and Tyrone giggled loudly.

'I know what you mean,' said the man. 'They play havoc with my bowels too! Do you boys live around here?'

'Yes. We live up the road next to Mrs Grumpold,' Orlando said.

'Never heard of her,' said the man. 'Right, what are your names?'

'I'm Orlando and I'm named after that place in America. He's Sylvester and he's named after Sylvester Stallone the Rocky boxer. And this is our little brother, Tyrone. Ma loves *Coronation Street*!'

The man **ROARED** with laughter. 'Your mum and dad have a great sense of humour. I *love* your names. Mine is Mr Dinsdale. Gregory Dinsdale. Everybody calls me Greg Green Fingers.'

'Why?' asked Sylvester.

'Because I'm always gardening.'

SYLVESTER LOOKED AT HIM OPEN-MOUTHED.

'Plants are *green*,' Mr Dinsdale pointed out.

'Oh,' Sylvester muttered, still none the wiser.

'I'll explain later, Sylvester,' Orlando said. 'Now what, exactly have we got to do, Mr Dinsdale?'

'I'll show you,' he replied. 'Follow me.'

He led them through the allotments and stopped at his own plot. There were loads of stalks with green golf balls growing on them. **THEY LOOKED LIKE SOMETHING FROM ANOTHER PLANET.** The boys stared at them, fascinated.

'Here we are,' he announced. 'My very own humble estate.'

'What are *those*?' Orlando asked, pointing at the weird plants.

'Sprouts,' Mr Dinsdale replied. '*They* are my sprouts.'

'Sprouts!' Sylvester responded. 'I've never seen sprouts like that. They are all stuck together!'

'That's how they grow,' Mr Dinsdale said with a grin. 'You have to cut them off or pull them off. Then you take them home and cook them and they are delicious.' He showed them how to hold a sprout and pull it off the stalk.

'I have never ever thought of sprouts as being delicious,' Orlando said grimacing.

'Nor me,' Sylvester agreed. 'What do you think, Tyrone?'

Tyrone pulled a face and hid behind Orlando.

'I tell you what, boys,' Mr Dinsdale continued, 'if you can pull off forty and put them into this bucket, I will buy you an ice cream each. How does that sound?'

'Brilliant!' Orlando cried.

'OK. Now if *you* do that, I can go and fill my watering can at the tap. It's at the other end of the allotment. I'll be about five minutes. Will you be OK to carry on without me?'

'Easy-peasy,' Sylvester said confidently.

Greg 'Green Fingers' Dinsdale collected his watering can, gave them each a 'high five' and left them to pull off thirty-nine more sprouts.

Orlando pulled one and **dropped** it in the bucket. 'That's two,' he counted.

Sylvester did the next one with some difficulty. 'These are tricky,' he grunted. 'This one is fighting back!'

They pulled off a further twenty when, suddenly, Tyrone yelled. 'Look! There's a rabbit!'

The boys looked up to see a **RAT** with a long tail going through the sprout stalks towards the Club House.

'That's not a rabbit,' Orlando called nervously. *'It's a rat!'*

They had never seen a rat in real life before, but they knew that people seemed to be **frightened** of them. 'Quick, get the catapults out of Tyrone's backpack,' Orlando said, taking command. 'This is our chance to be heroes!'

Within seconds, the first sprout was pinging its way towards the rat – fired by Orlando. It **BOUNCED** off the club house, missing the rat by only a few centimetres. The rat stopped in its tracks and looked at them.

They fired off a barrage of sprouts, but the rat was

on the move again. **THERE WERE SPROUTS BOUNCING EVERYWHERE!**

Sylvester took careful aim and fired. '*This time,*' he hissed through his teeth. He missed.

Then, out of nowhere, a ginger cat appeared and began to chase the rat. The rat *swerved*, followed by the cat and Orlando's next sprout smacked into the cat's shoulder. It let out a painful *yelp* and disappeared up a tree near the railings.

'Oh that poor cat,' he whispered.

The rat SHOT up the side of the club house and now sat on the window sill cleaning its whiskers with its paws. It seemed to be challenging them.

'*Let's get him, Orlando,*' Sylvester grunted angrily.

Just then, Mrs Chisholm came out of the club house with a cabbage and cauliflower in each hand. She turned and looked up just in time to see both boys fire sprouts. Sylvester's sprout **THUDDED** into the sill just under the rat and Orlando's sprout bounced off the sill and flew up into the air before dropping down into one of Mrs Chisholm's wellies. She squealed with fright.

Sylvester's next shot crashed through the window

with a resounding

CRASH!

The rat took off and disappeared into the bean canes.

The boys looked at each other with worried frowns and Tyrone put both his hands to his ears.

'I think we had better get out of here fast,' Orlando called. They grabbed Tyrone's hands and took off almost as fast as the rat and they did not stop running until they reached home.

Breathless, they ran inside and up the stairs to the peace and safety of their bedroom.

But there was another shock for them there! Ma had placed *all their toys* on their beds and left a note. It read:

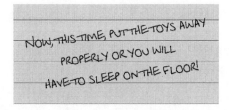

NOW, THIS TIME, PUT THE TOYS AWAY
PROPERLY OR YOU WILL
HAVE TO SLEEP ON THE FLOOR!

'*Pants!*' wailed Orlando. '*Pants! Pants! Pants!*'

CHAPTER SEVEN
Only Cows and Sheep!

'**O**rder! Order! Let's bring this meeting to order,' yelled Councillor Snodgrass, leader of the council. He banged his gavel down repeatedly on the wooden block.

Bang! Bang! Bang!

'Order!' he shouted. 'Order!'

The councillors began to settle down and, when the council chamber fell silent, he said, 'Madame Mayor, over to you.'

Everyone looked at Mrs Dulcie Tones, the Lord Mayor and she began to speak. 'I understand the passion that this family causes, but we must remind ourselves of our duty of care. We—'

The Lord Mayor was rudely interrupted by Councillor Frazzle. 'We shouldn't have to worry about that – they don't seem to care about anyone else!'

'Here, here!' shouted several council members. 'Here, here!' There were more MURMURINGS AND MUTTERINGS, and at least ten councillors waved their voting papers in the air.

'Madame Mayor, we don't need to be lectured on our duty of care to this family, and, may I remind you that we have a duty of care to *all* of their neighbours?'

'Here, here!' shouted loads of councillors. 'Here, here!' It sounded like a sheep farm!

'This family *must* be evicted again before we have a riot on our hands! The local residents are up in arms!' called an angry Councillor Banerjee. 'I thought we were supposed to be having a crackdown!'

'That's all well and good, Honourable Councillor but just *where* do we evict them to?' replied an equally angry Lord Mayor.

'May I propose Mars – on the next available space probe?' said Councillor Lightfoot.

There were **HOOTS OF LOUD, RAUCOUS LAUGHTER**; others shouted 'Here, here!' and some councillors even began to clap.

The Lord Mayor had to shout to make herself heard. 'Councillor, if you are not going to treat this situation seriously, then we are going to get *nowhere*!' she said dismissively. She heaved a sigh and looked at Councillor Snodgrass for support.

'Order!' he shouted and brought his gavel hard down on the block again. 'Order!'

'I *am* treating it seriously! I think Mars would be a great place for them as they would have no neighbours at all to upset!'

There was more laughter in the chamber.

'I second that motion,' yelled Councillor Barrito, laughing loudly.

'*This is ridiculous!* Of course we can't send them to Mars!' called Councillor Munching, chair of the council.

'Well, why not? It would get rid of our problem, wouldn't it?'

'We cannot send them to Mars because it would be *too expensive!* We have not got that kind of funding in our budget,' insisted Councillor Trotter, the Finance Officer.

'Oh, so the *only* reason we cannot send them to Mars is *cost!?*' said Councillor Frazzle, sneering. 'Balancing the books, eh?' she continued the assault.

'Precisely. No. I mean, no. *We cannot send them to Mars* because that would be *too drastic.* Inhumane! But you have just given me an idea,' Councillor Trotter continued.

'That's a first!' shouted Councillor Green. 'You've never had one of those before. I hope it doesn't give you a headache!'

The chamber **ERUPTED** into laughter once more and Councillor Trotter went red but, in spite of her embarrassment, she asked, 'Where could we send them where there are *no neighbours* to upset?'

'Mars!' shouted Councillor Merton.

'Councillor Merton, if you do not take this discussion seriously, you will be removed from the meeting!' said Councillor Munching disapprovingly.

Undaunted now, Councillor Trotter answered her own question. 'We send them to the *countryside.'*

She looked at everyone in the chamber. They were all silent now, staring back at her open-mouthed.

'Out in the sticks!' She searched their faces for a glimmer of agreement.

'Miles away from the city!' she called louder.

'Where there are only cows and sheep,' she added quietly.

'No people!' she yelled jubilantly. 'No... people!'

Councillor Trotter stared silently around every face in the chamber. No one moved. No one spoke. They all stared back at her in stone cold, silence. *This is unbelievable,* she thought.

Councillor Snodgrass began to clap. Slowly at first.

'No people!' Councillor Trotter repeated.

Councillor Banerjee joined in with the handclap. 'What a *great idea!*' he shouted.

A smile appeared on a few faces and slowly, very slowly, several others joined in and the **CLAPPING** began to get faster.

'Brilliant!' shouted Councillor Frazzle.

'Here, here,' muttered Councillor Green.

The clapping grew to a frenzy as almost every single one of the councillors joined in.

Councillor Barrito brought the euphoria to a sudden end by shouting loudly above the noise, 'Councillors, I am sorry to spoil the party but we don't have any houses out in the countryside!'

That took the smile off everyone's face and the chamber went quiet once more. Councillors looked around, searching faces for an answer to this troublesome family.

No one spoke until, 'Well, I suggest we buy one then. Fast!' called the Lord Mayor. 'Councillor Trotter. Get the accounts department to look into it straight away and buy a house miles away from anywhere, so that we can send them there. *'As soon as possible!'*

'Yes, Lord Mayor,' Councillor Trotter replied triumphantly.

'Oh, and Trotter...'

'Yes, Lord Mayor?'

'Buy a house *today!*'

'Yes, Lord Mayor.'

Councillor Snodgrass brought his gavel down hard and called 'Meeting Adjourned!'

Councillor Trotter looked at her computer screen with a smile, which became a grin, then a jubilant shout of, *'Aha! Got you my little beauty!'*

She had been searching **HOUSES FOR SALE** on the Internet for just over twenty minutes when she spotted exactly what she had been searching for. She studied the telephone number and carefully dialled the estate agent.

'Hello, can I speak to the person dealing with the house in Bosford Bliss please?'

'Who is calling please?' said the voice at the other

end.

'My name is Councillor Trotter and I want to discuss the purchase of Budleigh Cottage in Bosford Bliss.'

'Would you please hold the line and I will put you through to Mrs Evans?'

'Thank you,' said Councillor Trotter.

The phone went quiet for a few seconds then there was a **'click'** and a lady's voice said, 'Hello, Bronwen Evans. How can I help?'

'Oh, hello, Mrs Evans,' replied Councillor Trotter. 'Lilliana Trotter here. I am interested in the property in Bosford Bliss. It's called Budleigh Cottage, I think. Has it been sold yet or is it still on the market?'

'Well, there has been a lot of interest in it, but it is still available,' she replied.

'That's good,' she said. 'Can I put a deposit down on it *now*, please? *Today*?'

'Have you viewed the property?' Mrs Evans asked, rather shocked.

'Well, no I haven't, but I have read all of the details online and seen the photographs of the inside and outside of the house and, it is exactly what we are looking for.'

'That's very unusual, Miss Trotter. I am not trying to put you off but, I would strongly suggest that you view the house before making an offer,' Mrs Evans added.

'I understand your concern, Mrs Evans, but we have made our minds up on this. I'm calling on behalf of the city council and we want to purchase this house right now at the asking price.'

'Are you not going to haggle over the price at all, Miss Trotter?'

'No, we will pay the full asking price provided that the vendors will accept our deposit today. We want a fast completion. We need this house as quick as possible for one of our families to live in.' Lilliana Trotter smiled to herself.

'Well, I must say that this is extremely unusual, Miss Trotter, but if you are determined to purchase the property, I will contact the vendors right away and let them know. I'm sure they will be delighted with the news. Can I have your telephone number and I will ring you back in five minutes?'

Councillor Trotter gave her number and waited by the telephone tapping her fingers on the desk until Mrs Evans rang her back.

Twenty minutes later she was detailing everything to the Lord Mayor.

'Lord Mayor, it's done!' she said. 'The house is ours! I have paid the deposit by bank transfer and we only have to complete the paperwork now and pay the balance.'

'Splendid news, Lilliana,' said the Lord Mayor. 'Now, get Snodgrass to inform Mrs Shufflett and we can soon be rid of them *forever!* You have done well, Lilliana. This is a great day for everyone. A great day for the City.' She raised her fist high and brought it down to her chin with a long

'Yessssssssss!'

CHAPTER EIGHT
Back-in-a-Box

'*G*errup! I won't tell you again!' shouted Ma. She stood at the bottom of the stairs looking up. There was no movement.

'*Did you hear me?*' she yelled, aiming her anger at the children who were **slobbing** in their beds, refusing to move.

'They can hear you in *America!*' a voice from under the bedclothes yelled back.

'Wotchit, Orlando, or *you'll get a clip*,' she threatened. 'Now get down here *fast*. You've got two minutes or you'll be going to school without *any* breakfast.'

'I don't want any,' Orlando muttered.

'*What?*' came a voice from downstairs.

93

'I don't want *any* breakfast. I'd rather stay in bed,' he mumbled – very quietly – more to himself than to his overworked mother. She did not like to be back-chatted, so he didn't take the chance of being heard.

Reluctantly he called back, 'OK, Ma,' and slipped out of his bed. He decided to wake the others.

'Tyrone, Channing, Sylvester, better move. Sounds like she's on the warpath. We'll be late again,' Orlando warned.

'It's Sunday, innit? We don't go to school on Sunday,' said a small voice, buried deep under a duvet.

'Quite right, Tyrone. We **don't** go to school on a Sunday,' said Orlando, mimicking the voice with some sarcasm. He reached over and dragged the duvet completely off his youngest brother in the bunk bed next to him, and continued, 'but today's *Wednesday* and we *do* go to school on Wednesdays! *Unfortunately!*'

Tyrone squealed on his bed, and curled up into a ball.

Orlando stood up, stretched and yawned, picked up his own pillow and bounced it off Sylvester's head on the top bunk.

Smack!

'Get up!' he shouted.

Sylvester screamed like a wild pig, and leapt off the top bunk onto Orlando's head. Except that Orlando saw him coming and skilfully sidestepped **LIKE A MATADOR**. Sylvester landed on the floor, spread-eagled. He hissed like a boxer as the wind was knocked out of his lungs. He didn't shout. He lay there, wheezing and gasping for air just like a fish out of its tank; his mouth opening and closing.

'Is he trying to sing?' Tyrone asked.

'Nah, he's miming,' Orlando replied, inspecting the flapping body on the floor. 'There's no sound. He must be pretending; just like they do on the telly.' Sylvester was changing colour from red to purple as Orlando, with an imaginary microphone in his hand, began to dance and sing. Tyrone joined in, once he knew what to sing.

'I'm a little fishy watch me swim, here's my tail and here's my fin...'

Orlando stopped singing suddenly. 'I don't like the

look of him,' he said with some concern in his voice.

'Nor me,' said Tyrone. 'Tell him to keep his mouth closed. He looks much better when it's closed.'

Orlando bent down and helped Sylvester onto his back. 'Come on, sit up you fat fish!' he said, with a grin.

At that very moment, Sylvester swung his right arm around and **SMACKED** Orlando across the face. Then he leapt on him and began swinging punches. 'See how you like it!' he screamed.

'You little creep!' Orlando shouted from underneath Sylvester. 'You were putting it on all the time.'

Tyrone leapt on top of the writhing bodies hoping to drag Sylvester away from Orlando. He grabbed Sylvester's hair and YANKED hard.

'Aaaarghh!' screamed Sylvester. He jerked himself upright and fell backwards. It felt as though his little brother was removing fistfuls of his beautiful curly hair. He grabbed Tyrone's hand and tried to pull it away from his curls, jumping on top of him to get a better grip. **TYRONE BEGAN TO HOWL.** Orlando grasped Sylvester around the waist and, with a mighty effort, lifted him from the howling Tyrone. Sylvester immediately began to KICK at Tyrone with his flailing legs, and Orlando had to turn around, still holding an angry Sylvester off the floor, to save Tyrone from the kicking.

'Don't ever pull my hair again!' yelled Sylvester through gritted teeth.

Orlando put Sylvester down and held his arms out to stop him from leaping back onto Tyrone.

'Stop, now, Sylvester!' he grunted breathlessly. 'That's enough!'

Sylvester looked back at him **angrily**, breathing hard, trying to decide his next move.

Then, Tyrone, for some inexplicable reason, jumped onto Orlando's back – the way footballers do when someone has scored a goal! And Orlando fell on Sylvester with all three of them collapsing in a heap on the bedroom floor.

That would have been the start of a mighty scrap, but they looked up to see Ma standing there. **SHE WAS NOT HAPPY!** 'Get downstairs, eat your breakfast and *go to school!*' she roared. 'Let your teachers sort you out.' She held up a newspaper. 'Unless you want some of this,' she said brandishing the paper like a rounders bat.

All three of the boys fled past her to get downstairs, ducking as they passed.

They **raced** into the kitchen and within moments were sitting eating their porridge, in silence. Ma appeared several seconds later with Baby Beyonsay in her arms. Channing was behind her; washed dressed, tidy and carrying her school bag. She was the quiet one, although she wasn't frightened of her brothers. She could scrap as well as any of them.

'Why isn't Channing eating her breakfast?' Sylvester whined.

'For your information,' Channing smirked. 'I had my breakfast half an hour ago while you were still stinking in your pit! And I've been practising my spellings since then. Did you remember there's a test today, Orlando?'

'*No way!'* Orlando winced. 'It's not fair! They never give us enough time to learn our spellings properly.'

'You've had a week – the same as everybody else,' replied Channing.

'You see – *never enough time!* What do they expect of me? *I'm only a child!'* Orlando wailed melodramatically.

'Right! Move it!' hollered Ma. 'You three get upstairs and get dressed for school. I've got to feed the bab. And then I've got to go and see this bloke about moving house.'

EVERYONE FROZE LIKE STATUES and stared straight at their mother. Then, they all spoke at once.

'Moving house? What do you mean? We've only been *here* for five weeks!

'What for?'

'We were only at the last house for eight weeks!'

'What's going on?'

'When?'

'I like this house. I want to stay here. Why *can't* we stay here?'

'Where are we going?'

All these questions at once... everyone began talking... shouting... then the bab began to cry.

'Out!' yelled Ma and everybody moved.

 Fast.

CHAPTER NINE
Arthur and Margaret

Arthur. It was a name that didn't sound right if you shortened it. You just couldn't say 'Arth'.

'Arth, darling, pass the pickled onions.'

'Arth, come and get your tea.' It just wasn't right!

You had to say 'Arthur'. Arthur sounded perfect. **Powerful.** It worked.

But Margaret, that was different. Marg. Margo. Margie. Even Maggie. They stood efficiently as short versions and sounded OK too. You could use those short names easily.

But not if you knew her.

Margaret was not a Marg, a Margo, a Margie or even a Maggie. Margaret was... well... Margaret. No one ever called her anything else and, if you knew her, you would understand why. She was...

Cheerful.

Kind.

Caring.

Considerate.

Helpful.

Dignified.

Organised.

And quiet.

She would help anyone at any time. She was contented, and 'Margaret' suited her personality perfectly.

Margaret **LOVED** cooking and gardening, and keeping fit and healthy. She made cakes for everyone and grew more fruit and vegetables than she and Arthur could ever eat. SO, SHE GAVE AWAY THE REST.

If she wasn't gardening, she could be found in her sewing room making clothes.

Or at the Village Hall, helping with the Toddler's Group.

Or at the Women's Institute raising funds to help local charities.

She was a picture of health.

And, so too, was Arthur.

Arthur was an encyclopaedia. He knew something about nearly everything. He was an engineer and a handyman. There wasn't a machine in the village that he couldn't fix or operate. People came from all over the place to get things repaired by Arthur. **HE COULD BUILD WALLS AND SHEDS, MAKE FURNITURE, CRICKET BATS, AND EVEN BOATS.** He could design and build a complete bathroom or a kitchen – whatever you wanted!

Arthur loved doing things and fixing things, and he did it all with a smile on his face. He had a work shed – A PROPER WORK SHED, WITH TOOLS AND MACHINES for making and repairing anything.

Arthur and Margaret had lived in the village of Bosford Bliss for as long as they could remember. It was a beautiful quiet part of rural Wales, closer to the River Usk than the River Severn and not too far away from the magnificent Raglan Castle. They had always been there; known by everyone, and everyone loved them. They never upset anybody and no one ever upset them.

Many, many years ago, in a different life, Arthur had had a **COMPLETELY DIFFERENT JOB.** He had been a professional footballer for nine years with Birmingham City FC, a First Division football team – that's the same as the present day Premier League. He had been a good player until his injury. The knee injury in October 1979 which had cut short his career at the age of 28.

Birmingham City, known as The Blues, finished

third that season in Division Two above Chelsea. Colin Todd, Frank Worthington and Alberto Tarantini – a World Cup winner with Argentina – also played for Birmingham.

Arthur had played with and against some very famous footballers such as Geoff Hurst who scored a hat-trick for England in the World Cup Final of 1966, Bobby Moore England's Captain, Cyrille Regis, Denis Law of Manchester United and Scotland, George Best, Kevin Keegan, Kenny Dalglish, and Trevor Francis – the first one million pound footballer.

Wembley was his one regret as a player. He had never played there and he would have loved to have done so. But he did play in two FA Cup semi-finals. And lost both times!

Arthur and Margaret hardly ever mentioned their previous life in football to anyone in Bosford Bliss. It didn't seem necessary. They had moved away from the city and settled into a quiet life in the Welsh countryside where their lives were very different.

But, he never lost touch with The Blues and was a life-long season ticket holder going to every home game and many away fixtures also.

After a year or so, as he began to recover from his knee injury, Arthur had taken his refereeing exams and now enjoyed refereeing local teams during the football season.

Arthur and Margaret lived in a beautiful house called Oak Cottage in the Gwent countryside, with about one hectare of land. 'That's about two and a half acres in old money!' Arthur would joke to anyone who asked how much land they had. 'That's about the size of two and a half football pitches – two and a half Wembley's,' he would add if they looked blankly at him. One hectare was enough space for all of their animals, vegetables, the orchard and the wood.

The cottage was built, as its name suggests, near two **ENORMOUS** oak trees, the largest in the county. 'They are over one hundred and eighty years old,' Arthur was always delighted in telling people. Oak Cottage was very pretty and nestled in the shade of the two oaks and a large orchard. Damsons, pears and apples grew effortlessly on the trees and Margaret lovingly transformed this abundant produce into jams, pies, pastries, sorbets and ice cream. A small stream ran through the bottom of their orchard and away through the wood, down to their nearest neighbours' house, Budleigh Cottage some two hundred metres away.

There were fish, newts and frogs in the garden pond; squirrels, blue tits and robins in the trees, and a dog called Floss, who seemed to get everywhere.

Floss was a black and white working Collie, who was four years old. She was extremely intelligent, with an amazing understanding of how to make Arthur and Margaret happy. She was **INCREDIBLY** fast. She could round up sheep before they even knew she was there! She would sprint around as fast as she could, her tummy low to the ground, stopping suddenly like a statue. Then, she would pounce in a final sprint, encouraging the sheep to run through the gate that was being held open by Arthur. Arthur had not trained her to do this. She was so intelligent that she simply knew what to do. She loved to help and she loved to be praised. Her tail would wag wildly and enthusiastically, and she would answer back with a quiet 'Oomph!'

Floss had an incredible sense of smell and knew immediately when there were rabbits about. She would sniff the air with her nose held up high, emit a low 'Woof!', and take off as fast as she could to track down the intruders. She could detect a sausage sizzling over a mile away. She knew whenever a fox had strayed too close to the hen coop and would run backwards and forwards sniffing the scent and growling.

Arthur and Margaret also had six hens, four geese, three sheep and a cow called Maisie. The hens and geese produced loads of tasty eggs, and the sheep and Maisie kept the lawns and paddock beautifully trimmed. They were as good as any lawn mower.

All of the animals seemed to love Floss, and she looked after them like a Mother Hen looks after her chicks.

Arthur and Margaret loved where they lived. They often told each other that they would never want to live anywhere else. LIFE, FOR THEM, WAS PERFECT.

Bosford Bliss was exactly that. Bliss. A wonderful place to live.

So, when the new neighbours arrived, no one ever thought that it would be **the start of a war!**

CHAPTER TEN
Back on the Road Again!

'**I**'m sorry, Mrs Shufflett, there's nothing I can do. It's out of my hands now,' explained the weary councillor Snodgrass. 'The decision's been taken by the entire council. A unanimous decision. You've *got* to move house.'

Councillor Snodgrass sat at his desk, **PEERING** over his reading glasses, looking directly at Ma Shufflett. His arms were resting on the desk, with his hands CLASPED together in front of him; his thumbs seemed to be pointed at Ma's head like a double-barrelled shotgun. In the gap between his arms were a few sheets of paper, which he looked at before beginning to speak. He had the smallest hint of a self-satisfied expression on his face. He was trying to be serious, but

Ma could see that he was holding back a smile.

'But you *can't* keep moving us like this. I haven't finished unpacking the boxes from the last move yet. *We've only been here five weeks!* Every time we get settled, you move us on again. We're like nomads.'

'But it's the complaints, Mrs Shufflett, the complaints.' He paused, staring hard at Mrs Shufflett, then continued. 'Your children are wild, Mrs Shufflett! Wild! Only the other day, your eldest boy, Orlando, set fire to Mrs Grumpold's wig!'

'Yes, but he was trying to light her birthday candles, and there was a lot of them. She's sixty-eight, you know,' Ma remonstrated. 'One candle went out, and as he tried to relight it, she bent forward to blow them out. And *up she went like a bonfire*,' Ma added. 'But it wasn't Orlando's fault. He was doing his best.'

'OK, OK,' he said looking down at his notes, 'but what about the paint on the pavement, and the eggs on Mrs Mildew's windows?' he added. 'What about those?'

'I think you're picking on my boys. They're just friendly and like to help people out,' Ma said.

'*And* Mr Wegley's shed?' he continued.

'First of all,' Ma countered. 'Orlando was *helping* Mr Gamboll carry the paint into his house for him, but the tin was too heavy and it fell out of his hands. He couldn't just leave it there. Anybody could have slipped in it. I thought it was quite good of him really – to try to clean it up!'

'Yes, but he took Mrs Grumpold's tea towels from her line to clean it up with!' The man seemed exasperated. 'And I suppose the eggs *slipped* out of his *delicate little fingers* too?'

'That wasn't Orlando,' said Ma, tapping her foot. 'No. That wasn't Orlando. That was *Sylvester*.'

'Sivee!' squealed Beyonsay, looking up at Ma and smiling through her dummy.

'Yes, my little precious,' Ma said soothingly.

'He was only practising his bowling. He's getting better you know. He scored four out of six that time.'

Ma almost sounded proud and sat quite still, staring across the desk at councillor Snodgrass. 'He's going to be a cricketer when he grows up.'

Baby Beyonsay sat silently on Ma's lap playing with her doll. 'Sivee,' she called out.

'Good girl,' said Ma. 'It was Sivee wasn't it?'

MR SNODGRASS GLARED AND TOOK A SLOW, DEEP BREATH BEFORE CONTINUING.

'And what about the mess your boys made up at the allotments? Mr Dinsdale's sprouts were ruined. Your boys went to help him pick his sprouts for cooking...'

'You see!' Ma interrupted. 'I told you. My boys love to help folk.' **MA SEEMED PLEASED WITH HERSELF.**

'Really? How *were* they helping, exactly? Your beloved Sylvester was catapulting sprouts at Mr

Dinsdale's cat. The poor little thing; they still haven't found him, and another sprout broke the window of the clubhouse.'

'I think you're being very harsh on my boys,' Ma persisted. 'I thought the path looked much nicer painted blue. What about the time they went shopping for old Mr Wegley? Nobody said *thank you* for that, did they?'

'That's because they ate all the ham, cheese and crackers a*nd* a whole bar of chocolate before they even got back to him. The bag was *empty* except for the four candles.' Mr Snodgrass seemed to enjoy pointing this out. 'And *we* know what happened to *them*, don't we, Mrs Shufflett?'

MA LOOKED A LITTLE UNEASY. 'Well... I'm not sure I can... er... erm... remember,' she lied.

'Oh, let me help you. Mr Wegley told the boys to put them in the cupboard but, instead, they took them down to his shed, didn't they?'

'Yes, but Mr Wegley got a brand new shed out of it. He wouldn't have if—'

'If *your children* hadn't burned it down!'

'It was an accident!'

'They shouldn't have been in there in the first place!' Mr Snodgrass yelled.

'They called the fire brigade, didn't they?' Ma pointed out.

'Yes, they did – after it had arrived! And one fireman tripped over Sylvester knocking the television and a vase on to the floor, and then Mr Wegley slipped on the wet floor and banged his head on the TV.'

Mr Snodgrass was becoming redder and redder now. 'Poor Mr Wegley had to spend the night in hospital with a big lump on his head.'

'You can't blame my boys for all that,' Ma retorted.

Mr Snodgrass looked down at his notes briefly and continued. 'Mrs Shufflett, can I speak honestly here?'

'Of course you can,' Ma replied, 'but don't tell me we've got to move again.'

'If I never saw you or any of your family again, it would be too soon!' he said.

'Does that mean we can stay?' asked Ma hopefully.

'Not a chance!' Mr Snodgrass growled. 'Not a chance!'

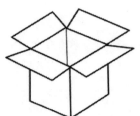

CHAPTER ELEVEN
Boxing Up Day

It was early spring. In Arthur and Margaret's garden the snowdrops had only just finished their beautiful display and had gone back to bed for another year, and it was the daffodil's turns to show off.

Next door in Budleigh Cottage, Edward and Doreen had finished their breakfast and, together, were washing up the dishes. As they did so, Arthur came **BOUNCING** out of the woods, across the patio and in through the kitchen door carrying cardboard boxes.

'Thought you might like these,' Arthur said as he let himself in through the door.

'Thanks, dear,' Doreen said. 'Would you like a cup of tea?'

'I wouldn't say no,' Arthur replied. 'Is there any

whisky to go in it?'

Doreen laughed. 'No,' she chuckled, 'but we've got loads of milk!'

Arthur smiled, removed his coat and placed it on the back of a chair. 'How's everything going? Are you ready for the big move?' Edward and Doreen were moving back to their childhood home in Portsmouth.

They had lived next door to Arthur and Margaret for almost thirty-two years (well, next door was over two hundred metres away on the other side of the wood, but they were next door neighbours just the same).

'Yes, it will be nice to live near the coast again and feel the sea spray on our faces,' Doreen said.

'If you get that close to the sea, you had better make sure that you've got your rubber ring and snorkel handy!' Arthur grinned, noticing that everything was labelled neatly. There was a big box labelled 'charity shop' and another 'rubbish tip.'

'Where's the box labelled "Arthur and Margaret"?' he asked feigning disappointment.

'Couldn't find anything to put in it, Arthur!' Edward said, laughing.

'A few five pound notes would have been OK to start with, Edward! Where's your imagination gone?' They all laughed.

'This looks *very* organised, Doreen,' Arthur continued.

'It is *now*, but you should have seen it yesterday. There was stuff everywhere. Trouble is, this all brings back a flood of memories.'

'Yes, look at this,' Edward said passing Arthur a battered photograph. IT WAS A PICTURE OF A BOY RIDING A BIKE.

'Remember this? It's our Charlie riding his first bike.'

'Oh, yes. If I remember correctly, he thought he could ride on his own till you let go of his saddle,' Arthur said with a smirk.

Edward winced, remembering the crash as Charlie hit the floor.

'He still has that scar,' said Doreen, interrupting them.

'True, but he didn't fall again!' Edward added. THEY ALL SMILED AND FELL SILENT AS THEY REMINISCED.

Edward took out another photo of Charlie. This time he was sitting on the branch of one of Arthur's oak trees. He was trying to save a cat and they both looked terrified! They all burst out laughing.

'Oh, I remember that day. We had to get the fire brigade to get them both down!' THEY ALL LAUGHED AGAIN.

'So, *who* is going to buy your house?' Arthur asked, changing the subject. He was intrigued by his new neighbours would be. 'I hope you've got someone nice to come and live next door to us. A famous film star or singer would be good.'

'Well, it's strange you ask,' Edward replied,

'because we've sold it to a city council many miles away from here. Can't think why they'd want to buy a house so far from their own city.'

'Yes, that certainly seems strange,' Arthur agreed. 'Perhaps they want it for the Lord Mayor.'

'The Lord Mayor?' Edward repeated. 'What would the Lord Mayor need our house for?'

'Oh, I don't know. Perhaps somewhere quiet for him to get away from all of his important duties. Have a rest. That sort of thing. A bit like the Queen when she goes to one of her other palaces!'

'Yes. I see what you mean. Who knows?' Edward said.

'Besides,' Arthur continued, 'Budleigh Cottage is big enough to hold the entire City council members for their meetings!' Arthur joked. 'But I hope they don't. I prefer the quiet life myself. Maybe he'll only be here at weekends,' he continued. 'It would be like not having a neighbour at all, wouldn't it? Mind you, Margaret is a bit worried,' he added.

'Why is that?' Edward asked.

'I'm sure she is!' Doreen interrupted. 'I would be *very* worried. Not knowing what the new neighbours will be like is a big worry to anybody.'

'Well, we will know soon enough,' Arthur said, finishing his cup of tea.

'I *do* hope you get someone really nice,' Doreen said thoughtfully.

'Yes.' Arthur laughed. 'Much nicer than the current owners, I hope!' HE DUCKED AS DOREEN THREW A WET DISHCLOTH AT HIS HEAD.

Arthur stayed for a further ten minutes to help Edward move a few heavy boxes. 'Well, it's time I went home,' he said. 'I need to take Floss for her walk. I'll leave you two to carry on with your packing. And, don't forget to fill a box of treasure for your poor old neighbours next door in Oak Cottage!'

'Not much chance of that, Arthur,' said Doreen. 'But you can have our old tea towels and Edward's sweaty socks.'

'Ugh!' muttered Arthur opening the door.

'Thank you for the boxes, Arthur.'

'Not at all!' he called back. 'Put his sweaty socks in one of *them*!'

CHAPTER TWELVE
Get Outta Town!

The bell rang.

Orlando heaved a huge sigh of relief. It was the end of another **BORING** day at school.

But for Channing it was different; she had enjoyed Maths and PE followed by a history lesson about Queen Nefertiti of the Ancient Egyptians.

In Literacy she had written three Haiku poems about spring:

	Spring is all around
Sunshine, snowdrops, birds singing	
	Make me feel happy

	At last new leaves grow
	Cherry blossom is in bloom
	Spring brings life and growth

	Warm sunshine morning
	Birds chattering in the trees
	Building nests for chicks

Miss Truman had read them to the whole class. Channing was so embarrassed by this and she went bright red.

Orlando, her twin brother, who was in the same class and had spent most of the day drawing pictures of his favourite superheroes, spotted her embarrassment. He began to grin, and pointed at her. Some other boys did the same. She stuck her tongue out at him, but felt betrayed and let down. *Why would her own brother be so cruel to her in front of others?* She wanted to go over to him and give him a **THUMP!**

Then she felt like crying; she just wanted to disappear and get away; to get out of the room. *Why are boys so stupid?* she thought. The more she thought about it, the redder she became! She knew that Orlando would tease her and torment her later. Probably for days. She dreaded the thought. Brothers. **Horrible brothers!**

'OK. See you all tomorrow, children,' said Miss Truman. 'And don't forget your homework for Friday.'

I won't be doing that, thought Orlando.

The children drifted out of the classroom into the cloakroom to gather bags, lunch boxes and coats. Orlando couldn't wait to catch Channing's attention.

Channing was chatting with two other girls and headed straight for her peg. She could see that Orlando was waiting for her and tried not to look directly at him. She busied herself putting her reading book and pencil case into her bag.

'Tomato face!' shouted Orlando. 'You looked just like a tomato. I've never seen you look so red.'

'Belt up!' said Channing.

'I could feel the heat from your face on the other side of the room. I nearly had to put sun cream on.' Several boys were laughing now.

CHANNING HAD HEARD ENOUGH. She thrust her way through the other boys who were laughing and put both her hands on her brother's chest and shoved him as hard as she could. 'Get lost!' she yelled.

Orlando was HURLED backwards. Before he could gather his footing, he tripped on his bag, landed on his back like a sack of potatoes and slid, on his back, along the floor. 'Aaargh!' he screamed as his head banged into the wall.

Miss Truman appeared and she was not happy!

'What's going on in here?' she demanded.

Channing looked at her but said nothing.

'Sorry, Miss,' Orlando groaned, getting up. A bump had already begun to rise on his head. 'I tripped over, but I'm OK.' Ma had always taught them to stick together, no matter what. And never, never, twit on each other. Funny he should remember that now!

'Did you hurt yourself, Orlando?' asked Miss Truman.

Orlando wanted to say, *'No. Why would I hurt myself? That's a daft question!'* but did not dare to say it.

'No, thank you, Miss. I'll be fine.' His head was throbbing, but he managed to force a smile.

Channing looked defiantly at him but was grateful that he had not grassed her up.

'All right, Orlando. If you are sure.'

'I'm good thank you, Miss. See you tomorrow.'

Miss Truman turned back to the classroom but did not go in. She stood by the door, watching the children leave the cloakroom.

Orlando and Channing picked up their bags and set off to collect Sylvester from his classroom. Orlando wanted to trip Channing over but could feel Miss Truman's eyes burning into the back of his head as they made off down the corridor, so he resisted. *I'll get you later,* he thought.

Sylvester was waiting **IMPATIENTLY** outside his classroom. 'Where have you two been?' he asked angrily. *'You're late!'* He was clearly not amused. 'I've been waiting here for ages.'

Channing looked at him FEROCIOUSLY but said nothing. Orlando would have laughed but his head hurt too much.

'Have you got everything?' Channing asked Sylvester. He nodded. 'Let's go then.'

The children sat in the kitchen and stared at Ma in astonishment. **No one spoke.** Until Tyrone finally broke the silence.

'We've got to move, *again.* Go to another house, *again?'* Tyrone asked, grasping the situation beautifully for a four-year-old.

'No, stupid!' replied Channing. *'They're going to give us a tent out in the back garden!'*

'I don't want to live in a tent,' whined Tyrone, who looked as if he was about to cry.

Channing opened her mouth to mince him into little pieces, but Ma yelled first.

'Right! That's enough! We've *got* to go and that's that,' she said firmly. 'And don't call him "stupid" again unless you want to be grounded for a week!'

'But I don't want to live in a tent,' Tyrone persisted, really crying now.

'Be quiet or you'll get a clip.' And she meant it! 'All of you start packing your stuff. We leave next Thursday.'

'It won't take me long to pack,' said Sylvester. 'I've only got my catapult and Spider-Man outfit.'

Ma glared at the children as they backed away out of the kitchen. 'We're going and that's final!' she shouted as they escaped into the living room.

CHAPTER THIRTEEN
A Sad Goodbye

Arthur and Margaret set off down their garden, through the orchard to the little stream, then turned and followed the stream through the wood, until they arrived at Doreen and Edward's back door.

IT DID NOT LOOK THE SAME. IT WAS COLD AND EMPTY. There were no pretty curtains in the windows. There was no washing blowing on the clothes line. No smoke came out of the chimney – and they could see right through the house from the back window to the front – there was nothing to be seen but boxes. Small boxes, large boxes, all taped up, with labels.

They decided to walk around to the front where the removal van was already being loaded. The men wore blue overalls that sported a large badge with:

"Ace Removals:
From Place to Place, you need Ace "

written on it. They all looked very busy carrying boxes from the house and loading them carefully on top of each other in the van. Furniture was covered in a blanket before it was carried out. Arthur and Margaret carefully walked through the front door, avoiding men, boxes and furniture.

'Hello, Doreen? Edward?' Margaret shouted.

'We're in here,' Doreen called back.

They found Doreen and Edward in the kitchen. Doreen was standing near the sink.

'This is the first time I've seen you by that sink without your yellow rubber gloves on, Doreen!' Arthur joked. 'First time in, let me see, thirty-two years.' No one laughed. THEY ALL FELT THE SADNESS OF THIS DAY.

Arthur saw tears in Margaret's eyes beginning to appear.

'Let's have a nice cuppa,' Arthur said. 'I've

brought some whisky to put in it.' Again, no one laughed.

'Is there anything I can help you with now, Edward?' Arthur asked.

'No,' he replied. 'Everything is done. We just have to wait for the van to be loaded. Then we can drive to our new home in Portsmouth. The van driver will follow our car.'

'Well, you have certainly picked the right day for moving,' Doreen said. 'Look at all this sunshine.'

It was a beautiful spring morning and they decided to have a final picnic together. They walked out onto the patio carrying cake, biscuits and drinks.

'It's a good job you're not taking this table with you, Edward,' Arthur joked as they sat around the picnic table and bench. 'Otherwise we'd be sitting on the patio!'

'We've decided to buy a new garden set for the new house, so we are leaving this one here. I'm sure the new family will enjoy it,' he replied.

'Is there any news of who's going to live here yet?' Arthur asked.

'Well, as you know, the Birmingham City Council bought the house from us,' Doreen replied.

'It will *not* be the Lord Mayor,' Edward said with a laugh.

'No – we had a letter from the council yesterday saying that they are sending a family from the city to live here,' Doreen continued.

'Yes. Some posh city people, no doubt. They'll be here tomorrow,' Edward added.

'Tomorrow?' Doreen said with a gasp. 'Did you say they will be here *tomorrow?'*

'Yes, tomorrow. The council needed to get them housed as soon as possible.' Edward replied.

'A big family, I believe,' Doreen said. 'The father works for the government or something like that. He's in the SAS. Never around much, apparently, always away on some secret mission,' she said.

'Won't they find it a bit quiet in the countryside?' Margaret enquired. 'We don't have things on the doorstep here like they do in the city. You know like cinemas, theatres, libraries, parks, shops or even pavements! I hope they don't get too bored.'

'It's possible,' Arthur said, 'but we came from the city and we didn't get bored, did we?'

'That's not *really* true, Arthur. Be honest. I wanted to go back home after two weeks if you remember. I didn't like the quietness, or the smell of the cows,' Margaret insisted.

'Yes, but things are different now, aren't they? There's the Internet and video games. They probably won't even notice that they're in the countryside. They'll be too busy on their tablet thingies. We probably won't see them very often,' Arthur continued.

LITTLE DID HE KNOW.

With increasing sadness, they finished their little picnic and went indoors to clear away the cups and plates. Two hours later everything was packed in the van. The Ace Removal men were sitting in the cab waiting for the signal to leave and Arthur was shaking hands with Edward. Margaret was hugging Doreen and telling her to have a safe journey and to stay in touch. And she was crying.

Doreen was saying that she *would* stay in touch and she, too, was crying.

The two men stopped shaking hands and turned towards the ladies. Arthur then hugged Doreen and Edward hugged Margaret, then the two ladies hugged each other once more.

The two men shook hands again – and couldn't resist a quick hug themselves. They had all known each other A VERY LONG TIME, so this was a very emotional moment.

'Margaret, living next to you and Arthur all this time has been... well, it has been...'

'A nightmare, Doreen! Go on – you can say it!' **Arthur interrupted and they all laughed.**

'Perfect,' Doreen continued. 'It's been perfect.' Doreen's eyes welled up and she smiled, dabbing away the tears.

'Oh, there's *bound* to be someone in Portsmouth who will upset you as much as I've done over the years!' Arthur joked and they all laughed again.

Doreen looked around one more time, studying Budleigh Cottage, their home for over thirty years. She sighed and turned to take hold of Edward's arm. She looked at Margaret, a tear in her eye. She shrugged and gave a final smile. Looking up at Edward she whispered, 'OK. Let's go. I'm ready.'

'Hang on a minute,' Arthur called. 'Let's have a final selfie.' He held his phone up high and they **CROWDED** around him for the last photo together. They all had to force a smile so Arthur shouted, 'Sweaty arm pits!' which made everybody giggle.

Then he took a picture of the two ladies and

Margaret took one of the two men.

'Let's have a photo of just you two,' Arthur said to Doreen and Edward. 'Come on, snuggle up close!'

Three minutes later, Doreen and Edward climbed into their car and they gave a tearful wave as the car pulled away. Margaret wiped the tears from her eyes as they disappeared down the long drive into the lane.

The last thing they saw was the side of the van above the hedge. **'Ace Removals. From Place to Place, you need Ace.'**

'Come on, my love,' Arthur said, putting his arm around Margaret. 'Let's go and have a nice cup of tea.'

'That would be lovely,' she replied.

'Your turn to make it,' they both said at the same time and laughed.

'I can't wait to meet the new neighbours tomorrow,' Margaret added. 'I should think they will be really nice, coming from the big city.'

'We'll see!' said Arthur quietly. 'We'll see!'

'I wonder what the children will be like,' she said thoughtfully. 'I know! I'll bake them a cake.'

CHAPTER FOURTEEN
Nearly a Dozen Eggs

It was a miserable morning. The sky was overcast and grey, and drizzle filled the air making everything feel damp. And it was cold. Despite this, **ALL THE RESIDENTS** had come out to see the Shufflett family evicted from their house. Seven members of the council had turned up too and were huddled beneath their umbrellas looking on intently. They each had a huge smile.

'This is one of the happiest days of my life, Mrs Frazzle,' said Councillor Snodgrass. 'It will be fantastic to get rid of that lot, and all the problems they cause.'

'It certainly will, Mr Snodgrass,' Mrs Frazzle replied, BEAMING. 'We have put up with them for long enough.'

Mr Snodgrass looked around at the other members of the council. They were all nodding in agreement.

'I still think we should have sent them to Mars!' said Councillor Lightfoot with a grin, and everybody laughed loudly.

'I'm worried for the cows and sheep,' said Mrs Frazzle. 'I think these kids will frighten them to death!'

'Well, thankfully, they are not our problem anymore,' Councillor Snodgrass added cheerfully.

Across the road four removal men were loading the Shufflett family possessions into the back of a removal van.

On the side it read:

**"Balvinder Transport
Any place – any time – any size."**

They wore white uniforms and carried boxes, a settee, table, chairs, wardrobes, a Spider-Man outfit, beds and more boxes and they were all wet with sweat and rain.

As soon as the furniture was fully loaded, Raj, the man in charge, headed back inside the house once more. Several minutes later he emerged, followed by Ma and baby Beyonsay. Ma held her head aloft and looked around at all the onlookers. Some were staring, a few were laughing, and one boy was JEERING.

There was a shout of 'Clear off you lot! We don't need you around here!'

Then a woman shouted, 'Good riddance!'

Ma glared at her, then smiled and kissed baby Beyonsay on the forehead. 'Look at all these lovely people,' she burbled gently. 'They have all come to wave us off to our new house. Yes, they have. Aren't they kind?'

'Kind,' Beyonsay copied her Ma.

'Clever girl,' Ma said, hugging her tightly.

She was followed by the rest of the Shufflett family. Channing read the situation immediately and her **HACKLES** went up. She was angry but put on her best smile. She raised her hand aloft and waved at everyone with the Royal wave – **just like the Queen.**

She was holding Tyrone's hand. He was wearing his wellies and backpack and was carrying Teddy.

'Wave to everyone,' Channing blurted out

through gritted teeth with a huge smile on her face. Her **LIPS DID NOT MOVE** as she spoke – she was just like a ventriloquist on the telly.

They waved majestically all the way down the path.

Orlando and Sylvester stepped out of the house together. Orlando held an imaginary gun and pretended to be shooting everyone, commando-style, squeezing **'Pff,'** through his lips with every shot. Several people ducked down when he aimed at them. 'Gotcha!' he shouted, grinning.

Sylvester held both arms aloft like the boxer, Rocky Balboa, after beating Apollo Creed. He grinned all the way down the path turning one way then the other to face **HIS ADORING FANS**, arms held high. Sylvester was named after Sylvester Stallone, the actor who played Rocky Balboa in the films.

He loved his name.

Raj was waiting at the end of the path and escorted them all to a minibus and instructed them to climb in and fasten their seat belts. They all climbed in, sat down and IMMEDIATELY IGNORED HIM – they were too busy looking out of the windows and **PULLING FACES.** Raj looked shocked then slid the door closed with a shrug and climbed into the removal van.

The driver of the minibus, Mrs Balvinder, turned round with a warm smile on her face and said in a gentle voice, 'OK, Mrs Shufflett, we have worked out the route and we are now ready to set off. Please could you all fasten your seat belts before we leave? It is very important.'

THEY ALL IGNORED HER TOO.

'Oh dear,' she said out loudly. 'This is going to be a *very* difficult time, I think.'

From behind several hedges along the road, heads **POPPED** up and faces peered out. Mr Wegley was standing on his front lawn with his dog, Herbie, sitting by his side. Herbie was **wagging** his tail excitedly.

'How's your new shed, Mr Wegley?' Orlando called out through the window.

'Very nice, thank you, Orlando. I've got an *electric light* now, so I won't be using any more candles,' he said, smiling back at the boys.

Mr Gamboll was leaning on his gate, just behind his beautiful, newly-painted blue footpath.

'You should paint the gate blue to match your path, Mr Gamboll,' Sylvester shouted. 'Would you like me to come and do it for you?' he added with a grin.

Mr Gamboll just smiled back and said nothing.

Mrs Grumpold's new blue-rinse wig was sticking up over her privet hedge. She thought that the Shuffletts could not see her there.

Mr Dinsdale and Mr Chisholm stood under a tree, while Mrs Chisholm was standing on her doorstep. A thick bandage covered her foot and she was holding a crutch for support.

Ma looked around at the scowling faces behind the hedges. She gave an angry stare back and all the heads popped down again.

'What are *they* looking at?' Channing asked angrily.

'Don't look,' said Ma. 'Take no notice of them. They're jealous of us 'cos we're going to live in the country.'

'Which country?' asked Tyrone.

'Shurrup!' said Channing. 'You're always asking daft questions.' Then she opened the window next to her seat and **PULLED** one of her best faces at Mrs Grumpold.

Ma gave Tyrone a big hug. 'She is upset, Tyrone, because we are leaving. She doesn't mean it. *Channing!* Tyrone does *not* always ask daft questions. Just *sometimes.* So, don't shout at him like that or you'll get a clip!'

'Sorry, Ma. Sorry, Tyrone,' she called back, still pulling a face at Ava Grumpold.

Mrs Grumpold ducked down behind the hedge. 'I wish they would hurry up and *clear off,*' she said loudly so that the other neighbours could hear.

It started to rain, but nobody wanted to go back inside until the Shufflets had gone.

'And me,' said Mrs Mildew. 'I'm getting soaking wet out here!'

'But there are no pigeons pooing on you now, Mrs Mildew!' shouted Orlando.

'Cheeky little monster!' she shouted back.

The council members walked across the road and stood at the side of the minibus. Mrs Balvinder started the engine. 'Please put your seatbelts on,' she said once more.

Mrs Mildew CAUTIOUSLY emerged from behind her privet hedge, still hoping not to be seen by the Shuffletts. 'What a horrible family they are,' she said. 'Look at the mess they've made of my house!' She pointed up at the dried remains of egg splattered across her window ledge.

Suddenly, **LIKE A BOLT OF LIGHTNING**, a cat scampered down from the tree and landed in Mr Dinsdale's arms.

'Dinky!' shouted Mr Dinsdale. 'You're alive and safe! Where have you *been*?' He cuddled the cat. 'I am

so glad you're OK.'

'Has he been stuck in that tree all this time?' called Mr Wegley from his front lawn.

'Yes, I think so,' replied Gregory Dinsdale. 'The poor thing! I think he was frightened of **THOSE KIDS NEXT DOOR** to Mrs Grumpold.'

'Goodbye, Mrs Shufflett,' said Mr Snodgrass through the open window of the minibus. He held up his hand to wave. 'I'm sure you will be very happy in your new house,' he added, almost grinning now.

'I'm not sure if your new neighbours are going to be so happy though!' said Mrs Frazzle with a laugh, and all the council members covered their mouths to hide their smiles.

They were all desperate to laugh.

Ma ignored them. 'Take no notice,' she told her children, but none of them were listening to her. They were all busy pulling faces through the windows.

Ma grinned and noticed that Beyonsay was falling asleep. *That will make the long journey a lot easier*, she thought.

'Seatbelts, please!' Mrs Balvinder insisted. 'We

cannot go until you all have your seatbelts on.'
Reluctantly, they buckled up.

Behind the minibus, Raj started the engine of the
van, flashed the headlights and gave a 'thumbs-up' to
Mrs Balvinder. She looked at him through her mirror
and gave a 'thumbs-up' in return.

With a **TOOT** of the horn the minibus began to drive
away.

Suddenly, to everyone's surprise in the minibus,
Sylvester leaned across to the open window and threw
two eggs with magnificent accuracy at Mr Snodgrass
and Mrs Frazzle.

Mr Snodgrass felt an **egg smash right in the
middle of his forehead.** Mrs Frazzle got one just
under her chin.

Both eggs began to drip downwards. Mr Snodgrass had egg yolk and broken shell in his eyes and on his rather large nose and moustache.

Mrs Frazzle felt her egg slide down the front of her dress. She squealed like a pig.

Ma looked and laughed, and the children cheered. Baby Beyonsay woke up with all the noise and began to cry.

'Drat!' said Ma and she cuddled the bab. 'Shh, I need you asleep on this journey,' she said gently.

'Great shot, Sylvester!' yelled Channing and Orlando.

As they made their way up the street, heads **POPPED** up above hedges just like ducks in a fairground shooting gallery. Everyone was waving and cheering at the departure of the Shufflett family. The council members were cheering and waving too. They were all so happy and relieved to see them go.

Sylvester had one more surprise in store. 'Open the windows, quickly!' he shouted, and Orlando and Channing leapt into action immediately.

Sylvester pulled out the rest of the box of ten eggs

and rapidly began to throw them, one at a time, at their former neighbours. Within fifteen seconds he had launched them all.

'Brilliant, Sylvester! Nine out of ten. You're getting better all the time!' said Ma and they all laughed. Even baby Beyonsay.

'Just exactly where are we going, Ma?' Channing asked.

'It's called Budleigh Cottage,' answered Ma. 'It's in Wales.'

SILENCE.

NOT A WORD WAS SPOKEN.

Until Tyrone said,

'Are we nearly there yet?'

CHAPTER FIFTEEN
RainDrops Keep Falling

Margaret came scurrying in through the kitchen door, slightly out of breath. She had just been out to feed the hens and geese, and it was raining.

'It's not very nice out there,' she puffed as she pulled the **DRIPPING** wet hood back from over her head and took her coat off. She shook it and water fell in small puddles on the kitchen floor. She hung it to dry on the back of a chair and went to check her hair in the hall mirror.

Arthur was busy making two cups of tea. 'Here you are, Margaret, just what the doctor ordered!' He grinned.

Floss, their black and white collie, came **BOUNDING** in from the snug, her tail wagging furiously as she sniffed around Margaret's wet shoes. She sneezed and snorted excitedly, skipping and dancing playfully at Margaret's feet. She was hoping for a biscuit or a nibble of something tasty.

'I fed the hens and opened the coop door but none of them seem inclined to go out. It's too wet and miserable for them,' she told Arthur. She studied the dark clouds overhead through the kitchen window. 'It's not going to be pleasant for the new family moving in,' she observed. 'Imagine having to unload all your furniture on a day like this! Ugh!' She shivered. 'It will *all* get soaked!'

'I'm glad we don't have to go out today,' Arthur said, carrying the two steaming cups of tea over to the kitchen table.

Floss **DANCED** about by their feet, waiting for a biscuit to be dropped her way. She was unlucky this time. There were no biscuits on offer, so she slinked, reluctantly, back to her basket in the snug.

As they watched, the rain began to fall harder, beating against the window pane.

Arthur finished his tea. 'Well, I can't sit here

enjoying myself, watching all this rain. I must go and get that rocking chair finished,' Arthur said. 'Mrs Balthrop, up at the Manor, would like it delivered tomorrow.'

He finished his tea and went out through the utility door leading to his workshop.

'I'll see you for lunch at one o'clock,' he added as he disappeared.

'Right. One o'clock it is. I will have some sandwiches ready. I think I will bake a cake for the new family,' she called after him.

Arthur walked through into his shed and immediately switched on a heater. He needed to get his workshop warm for the job he was about to undertake.

It was not really a shed. It was bigger than a shed. **MUCH BIGGER.** In fact, it was more like a small factory! AN ALADDIN'S CAVE. There were machines for everything he needed: a lathe, a drilling machine, a cutting machine, a router, grinding machines and a long workbench all the way down one side. On the bench were a variety of vices for holding things that he was repairing or making.

HANGING ON THE WALL WERE TOOLS OF ALL SHAPES AND SIZES.

There were machines for gardening, for building, for cutting down trees, for lawn mowing, for laying wooden flooring, and for making furniture. Under the work bench were piles of wood waiting to be made into something interesting for someone. There was wood of all lengths and sizes: some thin strips, some thick blocks and some planks. On a side wall there were boxes of screws – all neatly stacked in order of size and in plastic, see-through, containers. Next to the screws were the nails, all neatly boxed and ready to use. In the middle of the shed was a large empty space. This was where Arthur built the furniture or whatever he was making. In that space stood a rocking chair, ready for a final coat of varnish.

Arthur chose one of his softest finishing brushes and, using a screwdriver, he levered the lid off a tin of yacht varnish and set about the task of putting a final coat on the rocking chair. He turned on his radio for company, listening to his favourite music channel. Next, he turned the heater towards the rocking chair to blow warm air onto it, to help it dry more quickly.

In the kitchen, Margaret began making the cake for the new neighbours. It was to be one of her special double-layer sponge cakes with jam and cream in the middle and icing on the top. She worked happily and carefully, set the temperature of the oven, and was surprised when Arthur came in. Floss followed him, **RACING** in from the snug, hoping for a walk or perhaps a biscuit.

'Goodness is *that* the time already?' Margaret asked, wiping her hands on her apron, not expecting an answer.

'No, it's later than that!' Arthur replied, and laughed. 'Much later!' He began to wash his hands.

Margaret ignored his little joke and put on her oven gloves. She peered in through the oven window at the two sponge cakes inside.

Arthur studied the weather outside. 'It looks as though the rain is easing,' he observed.

Margaret was too busy examining the cakes. 'Perfect!' she exclaimed as she opened the oven door slowly to let out some of the heat. She waited as the heat dispersed before removing the first of the cakes. Carefully she placed the hot tray on the hob and inspected the cake thoroughly for any flaws. Satisfied that there were not any, she smiled, pleased with the outcome so far. Then she reached in for the second, and CAUTIOUSLY placed it side by side with the first.

'I'll let those cool down and finish the cake later,' she said out loud, more to herself than to Arthur, then took two mugs from the cupboard. 'I do hope they will like it,' Margaret said anxiously.

'Of course they will,' Arthur confidently replied. 'Everyone loves your cakes, you should know that.'

'I hope so,' Margaret said with some apprehension. 'And I hope they will be all right in the rain, too.' She poured the tea.

They sat down at the kitchen table to eat the sandwiches that Margaret had prepared, together with a nice cup of tea. Floss lay down at their feet hoping for some scraps to come her way.

Outside, the clouds burst open and the rain began lashing down again!

CHAPTER SIXTEEN
Act Naturally

Two hundred metres away, the Shufflett family were arriving at their new house. Mrs Balvinder turned the minibus off the lane into the drive leading to the house. The drive was about a hundred metres long and went slightly uphill, then downhill.

There was a wooden sign on a post. They all looked at the sign.

BUDLEIGH
COTTAGE

It was dripping wet in the rain.

'I can't see any houses down here,' Sylvester grunted, wiping the steamy window with his sleeve.

'I think it is at the bottom of the drive,' Mrs Balvinder called over her shoulder. 'Anyway, I hope so.'

They were almost at the end of the long drive when, suddenly, the minibus **vibrated violently** as though it had been shaken by a giant!

Brrrrrrrrrrrrrrrr!

Channing and Tyrone screamed, and Sylvester grabbed hold of Orlando.

'*WOW!* What was that?' Orlando yelled. 'Are we going to explode?'

'I'm sorry, I should have warned you,' Mrs Balvinder called to them all. 'That was a cattle grid we just went over.'

'What's a cattle grid?' Orlando asked immediately.

'Oh, it's a row of metal rails across the road that stops the cattle getting out,' she replied.

Orlando looked at Sylvester and they both decided that it would be worth having a closer look at the cattle grid later.

The family had been on the minibus for well over

one and a half hours and they were all irritable and frazzled. The **TORRENTIAL** rain was making things much worse. It had been about twenty minutes since they had passed the sign which welcomed them to Wales:

'Wow! Look at *that* dragon!' Sylvester called out.

'Are we really going to live in Wales now Ma?' Channing asked.

'Yes,' replied Ma. 'It won't be long before we are at the cottage.'

'How will Daddy know where we are?' Tyrone asked, looking a little worried.

'Don't worry about Dad,' said Orlando. 'He's a soldier. He will find us wherever we are.'

The minibus slowly drove downhill past a large pond on the left and, suddenly, a house came in sight.

A HUGE HOUSE!

'Wow! *Look at that!*' Orlando called. They all leaned over to get a better view.

'Is that Budleigh Cottage, Ma?' Channing asked incredulously.

Ma just stared without blinking. Beyonsay was asleep in her arms.

'I think it's a bit big to be a *cottage*,' Channing added.

'That's got to be two houses at least!' Orlando spluttered.

'According to my details, this is your new house,' Mrs Balvinder said. 'Budleigh Cottage.'

She drove towards the house and pulled up on a patch of open ground about thirty metres away from the path leading to the front door. 'I must leave room for Raj to get the van as close to the house as possible,' she explained. 'Otherwise, all your lovely furniture will be ruined by this rain.'

The rain pounded on the roof like an orchestra of drums. IT SOUNDED LIKE THUNDER.

'I'm not getting out in this!' said Channing.

'Nor me,' said Orlando looking all around him.

'*None of us* are moving 'till this rain stops a bit,' Ma said with determination.

Raj drove the van past the minibus and manoeuvred it, like an expert, into the space right in front of the house, backing it up as close to the path as he could. There was a hiss of brakes as he turned off the engine. He looked over at Mrs Balvinder, who pointed at her watch, then the sky, indicating that they should wait for a few minutes for the rain to ease. Raj gave a thumbs-up back.

'I spy with my little eye, something beginning with "b",' said Sylvester, feeling that now was a good time to cheer everyone up.

'I know,' Tyrone replied. '*House*,' he added with delight.

'Duh!' murmured Orlando, slumping down in his seat.

'You're *so stupid*!' Channing blurted in her usual exasperated way.

'Don't talk to your brother like that,' Ma said, 'or *you'll get a clip*,' and that was the end of that game!

The rain continued to fire little missiles down on

the roof. Then, slowly, the noise subsided to a gentle hum.

'I think that the rain is beginning to slow down,' Mrs Balvinder observed, looking upwards at the sky.

'I will get Raj to open the front door for you so you can all go into your new house.' She rang him on his mobile but, even before Raj had a chance to answer his phone, Orlando made his move.

'This is going to be amazing!' Orlando shrieked. He slid open the side door and deliberately leaped out into a **MASSIVE PUDDLE.**

It was like a bomb exploding! Water cascaded everywhere; over Orlando and through the open door. Ma felt the cold water splash over her feet and pulled

Beyonsay closer to her.

Orlando jumped again.

SPLASH! Orlando shrieked!

When did I ever get a chance like this before? he thought.

Sylvester could wait no longer and jumped off the bus. The dirty brown water instantly soaked him to the skin. He gasped at the coldness and it dripped off his nose and chin.

Orlando **SCREAMED** with delight and, by this time, was coming down for his third bomb blast.

Inside the bus Ma shouted, 'Pack it up you two or we'll all be soaking wet!'

Tyrone decided to get out and stood up to leave

with a huge grin on his face.

'Don't you *dare* move a muscle!' said Ma, growling at him.

Tyrone looked devastated and sat back down disconsolately.

Sylvester jumped high and came down in a puddle near Orlando. Orlando felt the **COLD** water soak through his clothes and laughed loudly. 'I'll get you for that, Sylvie,' he said grinning, and kicked a huge puddle at him. The spray was like a waterfall.

Sylvester squealed, kicked spray back at Orlando and shouted, 'Tyrone! Come on, it's fun!'

Tyrone dashed for the door.

'Get back here!' shouted Ma, but it was too late. Tyrone was already splashing up and down in his first puddle.

Bounce...

SPLISH!

Bounce...

SPLASH!

Bounce...

SPLOSH!

Like a family of kangaroos, they all jumped from one muddy puddle to the next. They were **SOAKING WET**, trying to soak each other, and having the time of their lives!

'Come on, Channing!' they shouted. 'Come and join us. *This is brilliant!*'

Channing looked at her mum hesitatingly. 'Oh go on then,' Ma conceded. She had never seen her boys having so much fun before – *ever*. 'Go on, before I change my mind.'

Channing was out of the bus **in a flash** and was dancing and splashing in all the puddles. This was sensational! Within seconds, she was drenched!

SPLISH!
SPLASH!
SPLOSH!

She jumped up and down. Up and down. She had never done anything like this before. It was still raining but none of them noticed it.

'I think your children are going to like it here,' said Mrs Balvinder to Ma. 'They seem to be having a great time already.'

'Yes,' Ma replied, 'but I don't know how I'm going to clean and dry their clothes!'

Nearby, Orlando noticed a wooden pontoon landing area jutting out into the pond. It was covered in green moss and looked as slippery as a greasy pole, but, **HE HAD NEVER SEEN A GREASY POLE**, so he did not know how slippery it would be! He ran over to it and stepped out into the middle of the platform and **LEAPT UP AND DOWN**, hoping to make it rock in the water, but instead his legs shot out from under him. Kicking and yelling, he plunged backwards into the murky water...

SPLADOOSH!

... and disappeared completely, except for his feet

which stuck up like two submarine periscopes.

Seconds later he stood up, **gasping** for breath. He was covered from head to waist with slimy green moss and pondweed. His dignity was ruined and he looked like **A GREEN MARTIAN**. He could not see a thing! Pondweed clung to his face and covered his EYES, NOSE AND MOUTH making it difficult to breathe.

Channing was hysterical! She was laughing so much that she too was struggling for breath. Sylvester wanted to laugh but did not dare. He knew that Orlando would be very unhappy if *he* did.

Tyrone began to cry. 'Orlando! Orlando! Are you all right?' he shouted. He was very frightened.

Ma, who had been focused on baby Beyonsay, could not see what was happening due to the large bushes blocking her view. **SHE COULD HEAR TYRONE CRYING AND BECAME ALARMED.**

Mrs Balvinder said, 'Please, let me help. Give me the baby, while you go and see what is happening.'

'That's very kind of you,' Ma replied and gave baby Beyonsay to her.

She stepped off the bus and cold water immediately

filled her shoes. 'Ugh!' she muttered. She squelched her way to the pond where the green alien, with long, green, flowing hair, was just climbing out, onto the muddy bank. It seemed to be heading towards Channing, who was laughing hysterically. Tyrone was still crying.

Ma took a few quick photos on her mobile.

The alien stood up at the edge of the pond and carefully moved the green hair away from his face and immediately became Orlando again. Tyrone began to smile through his tears. He was clearly relieved and Ma began to chuckle. THE CHUCKLE TURNED INTO A LAUGH AND THEN BECAME A HOOT LIKE AN OWL.

Ma and Channing were **LAUGHING SO MUCH** that they could not stand up straight. They leaned on each other for support.

They **shrieked...**
And **snorted...**
And **shrieked...**
And **snorted...**

And this only caused them to **SNORT** and **SHRIEK** even more.

Orlando began to walk towards them with his arms held out straight in front of him, like a **MUMMIFIED** monster. He was starting to see the funny side of this. 'I suppose you think this is funny?' he spluttered.

Ma and Channing shrieked again.

'Oh very funny, ha, ha, ha!' he added in a deep booming monster voice.

'The alien speaks with forked tongue,' Ma said, remembering back to The Lone Ranger and Tonto. 'I haven't laughed so much in years. Come on, alien. Let's go and get you cleaned up. Mind you, I think you'll need a haircut too!' AND THEY SHRIEKED AGAIN.

Ma led the way to the house with her arm around Orlando. Tyrone held Orlando's hand. They all stopped and looked up at Budleigh Cottage in disbelief.

'Oh my goodness,' Ma whispered, 'it's massive!'

'It's like Buckingham Palace!' Sylvester shrieked and ran down the path to be the first inside. *'I'm first in!'* he yelled.

Raj and the men had begun to unload the van as it had finally stopped raining.

Half an hour later, they were all wearing warm, dry clothes and Orlando was **BORED.** Ma insisted that they were to remain in the lounge until everything was in its correct place. The removal men were busy carrying furniture into the house and Ma was busy telling them which rooms to put it all into. She began organising the lounge and kitchen, opening boxes and arranging crockery and cutlery into various drawers.

'This is boring!' Orlando sighed. 'Let's go and see if there is anything exciting to do around here,' he murmured to Sylvester.

'Ma said to stay here in the lounge,' Channing reminded them but, they were not listening. They sneaked out through the open front door. Channing tutted. 'You'll be sorry!' she called after them.

Raj and the men were carrying boxes, pictures, mirrors, lamps, beds and furniture into all the rooms. Occasionally, they would check with Ma which room a particular item should go into. THERE WERE SO

170

MANY ROOMS.

The Shuffletts had never lived in a house with so many! There were five bedrooms, a kitchen, a utility, a shed, a wood store, the large lounge, a dining room and a snug **(A LITTLE COSY ROOM)**. Channing and Tyrone went into the kitchen to help Ma unload boxes.

'We've come to help, Ma,' she said.

'Where's Orlando and Sylvester?' Ma asked as they came through the door.

'They went exploring Ma,' Channing replied picking up some tins of soup and placing them in a cupboard.

'They'd better not get into any trouble, or they'll get a clip,' Ma mumbled.

Outside, Orlando and Sylvester had CREPT around to the back of the house and found a small stream leading into the pond. They followed the stream up through a steep wood until they arrived at a huge orchard. Beyond the orchard, they could see a house and some kind of shed.

They sneaked their way, **COMMANDO-STYLE**, up towards the shed and saw that it was inside a large fenced off compound. There was even wire fencing for a roof over the whole compound.

'What do you think is inside there?' Orlando asked his brother.

'No idea!' Sylvester answered. 'Could be a large rabbit hutch.'

'You're mad!' Orlando jeered. 'Rabbits don't grow that big!' He grinned at Sylvester. 'Come on, let's have a look.'

The door was made of the same wire fencing, with a wooden frame. Orlando opened the door and they crept inside the compound. He opened the door of the wooden hut and instantly there was a cackling and clucking of hens which frightened them both at first. SEVERAL HENS FLUTTERED THEIR WINGS FUSSILY.

'This place stinks!' Sylvester said, screwing up his face.

'Hens!' Orlando said, grinning. 'I've got an idea.' He reached out to pick up the nearest hen. The hen **CACKLED IRRITABLY** and flapped its wings. Orlando grabbed it with both hands and tucked it under his arm.

'You get one, Sylvester,' he encouraged his brother and, a few minutes later, carrying one under each arm, Orlando was **CREEPING** out of the hen coop. Sylvester could only manage one hen, but was able to close the door behind them.

There was no one in sight so they set off back to Budleigh Cottage. They had reached the stream and were heading downhill when, behind them, came a terrifying sound. It was like **several car horns blasting away** at the same time.

They looked around to see four huge geese running towards them screaming and tooting. THEIR WINGS WERE SPLAYED OUT WIDE AND THEY WERE ANGRY!

The two boys glanced at each other in terror, then ran for their lives. They hung on to the hens, little realising that this was the reason the geese were chasing them.

Down through the woods they raced, **slipping** and **SLIDING** in the mud, towards the safety of Budleigh Cottage.

*

Two hours later they were all waving 'Goodbye' to Raj, his team and Mrs Balvinder when Ma said, 'Right, let's go and get sorted.'

'Just a minute, Ma,' said Orlando, watching the Balvinder family head towards their vehicles.

'They're going to have a nice surprise,' Sylvester announced.

'Who is?' queried Channing, studying both boys with suspicion.

'Yes, *you two!* What is going on?' Ma growled.

'Just watch. That's all I'm saying!'

# CHAPTER SEVENTEEN
Tug of War

argaret was washing up the lunch dishes and Arthur was wiping them. Floss was bored and wanted some **FUN**. She suddenly appeared from nowhere and leapt at Arthur's trouser leg, gripping firmly with her teeth. She tugged hard several times and began to back up, growling gently. Arthur almost went flying and was balancing on one leg, trying to dry a plate. He **LAUGHED** out loud and Floss gave out another **'GRRR'** as she tugged at his trousers. She wanted some fun and tugged even harder.

Arthur hopped to the cupboard and placed the plate safely inside.

'I wonder how the new family are getting on,' said Margaret as she placed another dripping, steaming plate onto the draining board, completely ignoring the skirmish going on by her side!

'I expect they are getting very wet,' Arthur grunted breathlessly. 'It cannot be easy moving all their furniture in this rain. It's not very easy drying the dishes balancing on one leg either!' he said, waving the tea towel and looking a little helpless as he hopped back to the draining board for the next plate.

He wiped the plate and began to manoeuvre his way back to the cupboard to put it away, BUT FLOSS HAD OTHER IDEAS! She tried to tug him the other way.

Margaret, who had seen this happen so many times before, knew that Arthur was not going to get away without a battle. So, in order to save Arthur from serious injury – and his trousers from serious damage – Margaret collected one of Floss' tug-of-war toys and handed it to Arthur. He accepted it appreciatively and blew his wife a grateful kiss.

Still balancing precariously on one leg, Arthur dangled the tug-of-war rope in front of Floss' eyes. Floss was delighted and, in one flash of movement, she let go of the trousers and took a firm grip on the rope instead. This was now going to become her favourite game.

Arthur now planted both feet firmly on the ground and **TUGGED** on the rope. Floss pulled back with little bursts of energy. She had the rope firmly between her teeth and was not going to give it up without a fight. Her front legs were locked straight, with her paws anchored to the floor and her chest low down. She kept pulling backwards in little tugging movements trying to **WRESTLE** the rope away from Arthur who heaved the rope from side to side to shake Floss off, but this only made her bite harder without tugging. When he stopped this, she began the tugging movements again. Then, unexpectedly, Floss let go of the rope! This caught Arthur off balance and he fell backwards onto his backside.

'Aargh!' he cried with embarrassment and surprise. Floss had outsmarted him and now she pounced on him like a tiger. She put her snout into his neck and began nibbling at his shirt collar. Arthur could feel her cold wet nose on his skin as she moved from one side to the other. **SHE WAS RELENTLESS IN HER ONSLAUGHT.** This was her way of showing her affection and Arthur loved it.

Arthur was helpless with laughter now and becoming covered in **SLOBBER.** Every now and then she snorted to clear her nose as dogs do, and covered Arthur with even more **SLOBBER!** As he went to grab her, she moved to his other side and began again.

'OK, I've had my wash already this month and I don't need another.' Arthur LAUGHED as he began to get up.

Floss sat there looking up at him in a way that only dogs do. 'Woof,' she barked.

'I know. I know. You want a biscuit, don't you?' Arthur asked.

'Woof,' she answered again and moved slightly closer to him without actually lifting her backside off the floor.

HER TAIL BEGAN TO WAG.

She knew.

Arthur reached for Floss' dog biscuit barrel and took out a huge bone-shaped pink biscuit for her.

HER TAIL WAGGED EVEN FASTER.

'Give me your paw,' Arthur requested.

With no hesitation she did as she was told. Arthur shook hands with her paw. 'Good girl!' he said.

SHE SAT VERY STILL NOW.

No movement.

SHE DID NOT EVEN BLINK HER EYES.

Her complete concentration was on the biscuit in Arthur's hand. She licked her lips in anticipation and Arthur gave her the biscuit.

Floss took it so gently that you'd be forgiven for thinking that it was a delicate newly-born chick. She turned and went to find her favourite place in the snug to savour it in peace.

Arthur washed his hands and face, and carried on putting away the dishes.

CHAPTER EIGHTEEN
Keep on Running!

The rain had finally stopped and the day reluctantly began to cheer itself up. The Shufflett family stood on the doorstep saying 'Goodbye' to Raj and the rest of the Balvinder team. Mrs Balvinder smiled at Ma. 'I think you will be very happy here. It is a very nice house.'

Ma was holding Beyonsay and smiled back. 'I hope so,' she said. 'I very much hope so. It can't be any worse than our other houses.'

Mrs Balvinder put her hands on Beyonsay's cheeks and gave her a **KISS** on her forehead. Beyonsay **giggled**.

Then she **hugged** Ma and said, 'Goodbye, and good luck to you all,' and set off towards the minibus.

'Bye, and thank you for all your hard work,' Ma

called.

Sylvester smirked. 'They're going to have a nice surprise,' he said.

'Who is?' queried Channing, studying both boys with suspicion.

'Yes, *you two!* What's going on?' Ma growled.

'Just watch. That's all I'm saying!' Orlando stood grinning.

'What have you done?' Ma asked.

'You'll see... anytime now...' he answered, looking and waiting intently. 'Wait... watch.'

At that very moment, Raj opened the van door and began to climb up into the cab.

Immediately, two hens **FLEW** out past his head, cackling and clucking and flapping their wings wildly. Raj **ducked** and fell backwards to land on his bottom in the mud! Sitting there, he watched as the hens flapped unceremoniously to the ground, with tufts of feathers floating down behind them.

'Oh my goodness!' muttered Ma.

The children laughed. Even baby Beyonsay.

Getting to his feet, he turned and shook his fist at

the two boys. They grinned and shook their fists back at him.

Raj wiped his backside with his hand. It was soaking wet! **AND MUDDY!** Raj grimaced. 'Ugh!' he scowled.

Everyone was laughing now. Even Ma.

Raj reached inside the cab behind his seat and pulled out a cloth. He wiped the mud and water off his hand and bottom, and then shook his fist at the boys again.

They shook their fists back at him.

Thinking that this was the end of the incident, Raj climbed into the cab once more. Seconds later, he **LEAPT** back out again followed by a third hen which managed to land on his head before flapping down to the ground to join the other two hens.

Sylvester and Orlando were hysterical.

Raj rubbed his head with both hands in case there was any hen poo on it, then he wiped his hands on his cloth. 'Is that *it* now?' he called to the lads. 'Or are my wheels going to fall off?'

'Nah. I wish we had thought of *that* though!'

Orlando retorted.

Raj laughed and **SWUNG** himself up into the cab and closed the door. The other three men had missed this kafuffle, walking around the far side of the van, and now climbed into the other side of the cab. They stared at Raj. *'Don't ask,'* he said through **gritted** teeth.

Everyone laughed and Ma said, 'Come on. Let's go in and sort out the bedrooms.'

'Er... not yet, Ma. Hang on a bit longer,' Orlando said.

'What now?' Ma demanded suspiciously.

Mrs Balvinder had now reached the minibus. With a smile on her face, she opened the door and climbed into the driver's seat.

Suddenly, she leapt out again **SCREAMING**, with a look of sheer terror on her face! She was followed by a goose, **SQUAWKING** and **HONKING** like an old car horn. It stretched up to its full height and noisily began flapping its outstretched wings, all the time hooting a belligerent war cry.

HONK!

HONK!

HOOT!
HOOT!

Then it set off to chase Mrs Balvinder and she ran around the other side of the minibus to try to escape from its wrath. Three more **ANGRY** geese poured out of the minibus and joined the chase of the panic-stricken driver, their wings flapping out sideways, **BLOWING, TOOTING AND BLARING**. They really seemed to be telling her off!

Orlando and Sylvester were absolutely **hysterical** again. This was one of their very best pranks – *ever!*

Everyone was laughing. Even Ma. She could not help it.

Mrs Balvinder completed two circuits of the minibus before she was able to create enough space between herself and the geese to jump back into the driver's seat and **SLAM** the door behind her. The geese continued to leap up at her window, still squawking, hooting and flapping their wings.

Puffing and panting, Mrs Balvinder took several deep breaths until her pounding heart began to slow down.

Ma looked on nervously. 'Are you OK?' she called.

Mrs Balvinder gave her a 'thumbs-up'.

'Would you like a cup of tea to calm your nerves?'

Mrs Balvinder shook her head and gave an 'OK' sign with her thumb and fingers.

Then she began to giggle.

The giggle became a loud laugh, and then she turned to face the family and pulled her funniest face. Everybody fell about laughing and pulled equally funny faces back. Even Ma, but not baby Beyonsay.

Not wanting to be left out, Raj and the other men joined in too.

They didn't notice Arthur and Floss standing at the end of the drive, a hundred metres away, watching these crazy antics.

Once they had finished pulling faces and laughing, they all waved and the two vehicles drove off down the lane. By this time, Arthur had headed back to Oak Cottage.

Ma said, 'Come on. Let's go in and sort out the bedrooms.

# CHAPTER NINETEEN
Walkies

In the snug, away from all the pandemonium taking place next door, Floss was having a little **SNOOZE** on her blanket. She had no idea what was about to happen.

'I think I will take Floss for a **W. A. L. K.**' Arthur said spelling out the last word. He did not want Floss to hear it yet because she would get too excited before he was ready for her.

'She will need a bath when she gets back,' Margaret pointed out. 'Try to keep her out of the muddy fields if you can.' Margaret was sitting in her favourite chair in the snug, working on her latest cross-stitch picture.

'That's like asking her not to bark when she sees a cat,' Arthur replied. 'I'll do my best.'

Arthur used to say, 'Come on, Floss. Let's go for a lovely walk down the lane', or simply 'Walkies.' But he knew it was completely unnecessary these days. He **RATTLED** her chain lead and smiled, waiting for the whirlwind. Floss leapt up immediately, barking wildly, her tail wagging so hard that her body swerved sideways with each wag. She began turning in circles, all the time yapping and yelping, woofing and chatting.

Arthur sat on the chair in the hall and swapped his slippers for green Wellington boots while Floss leapt about around him. **HE STOOD UP**. 'You don't like going for walkies, do you?' Arthur smiled and he held up her collar. Floss stopped instantly and sat down looking up at him. She made a HUMMING sound and tilted her head from one side to the other. He pushed the collar over her head and said 'Wait!' FLOSS WAITED OBEDIENTLY, LOOKING UP AT ARTHUR. 'Heel,' he said and turned towards the door. Floss followed him, close by his left leg. She sat and waited as he opened the door. 'See you in half an hour, my love,' Arthur called to Margaret.

'Enjoy,' she called back. The door closed behind them, and Margaret left her cross-stitching and went into the kitchen to set about completing the cake for the new neighbours. She had decided to cover it with an icing sugar picture of their new house with the word **'Welcome'** underneath.

As they made their way through the front garden and down the drive Floss was glued to Arthur's left heel. They walked to the lane where Arthur stopped, and Floss immediately sat down on the **COLD, WET** ground. 'Ugh! I'm glad I don't have to sit down in this wet!' he said and bent down to release the collar. 'Wait!'

He looked each way along the lane. There was never much traffic but he always checked, just in case.

The lane was bordered on both sides by hawthorn hedges. Even though they had not begun to grow much this year, they were still far too tall for Floss to peer over but, in some places, Arthur was able to look over them across the fields to the church.

Floss waited for the command. They both waited, looking at each other.

'OK. Off you go!' he told her and she took off down the lane like a greyhound. Arthur followed but not quite as quickly. Suddenly she stopped and ran back a few metres and began sniffing the grass and stinging nettles at the verge. She **YAPPED, SNIFFED** and took off again searching for more yummy smells.

They made their way down the lane until they'd almost reached the drive leading to where Edward and Doreen used to live. Budleigh Cottage.

SUDDENLY, FLOSS FROZE, listening, not moving a muscle. Arthur stopped too. He cocked his ear just like Floss.

The noise coming from the long drive was not what Arthur had expected. The hedge here was too high for him to look over so he ran the last few metres to the entrance to the drive and stared towards Budleigh Cottage in disbelief. He could see two brown hens flapping away from a large removal van, with a man sitting down in the mud! The hens were **clucking, clacking** and **flapping** their wings as though they were in a great hurry. The man stood up and wiped the mud off his bottom, then began to climb into the van just as another hen leapt out of the van on to his head!

Three other men were beginning to climb into the other side of the van.

Beyond the van, a woman was running around a minibus. Arthur watched incredulously and then saw the reason why she was in such a hurry – four geese were **CHASING** her, and they seemed to be very angry for some reason.

There are no hens or geese around here except for my *hens and geese*, Arthur thought.

Just at that moment, the woman leapt into the minibus and slammed the door shut. The geese were now trying to jump up at her; they seemed determined to give her a piece of their minds.

Arthur had never seen anything like it. He stood

watching, amazed and **FLABBERGASTED.** Floss looked up at him as if waiting for her orders. 'Come on, girl,' he said gently, and was about to turn and walk on when something strange happened. The minibus driver pulled a face at the people standing on the doorstep. And all the people on the doorstep pulled faces back!

'All very strange, Floss,' Arthur said. 'Come on, let's go home and have a nice cup of tea.'

Instead of walking on down the lane, as they usually would, Arthur headed back home – to the huge disappointment of Floss.

On their arrival back at Oak Cottage, they were greeted by three hens, **clucking** and flapping over the fence. The hens went straight into their coop and continued **clucking** and flapping, as if telling the other hens about their little adventure.

Arthur looked across the field. He could see that the minibus and van had driven away and there were four geese racing headlong towards him. He watched them fly up gracefully over the fence and glide down to the pond where they settled quietly.

How did they all get into next door? he wondered.

They've never done that before.

He **STAMPED** his boots to clear off any mud and went in through the side entrance, where he had built a wet area for such days as today. Floss followed him grimly. She knew what was coming next. Arthur took the hose sprayer and sluiced off the remaining dirt from his wellies. Then he looked at Floss.

'Come here, girl,' he said kindly.

Floss put her tail through her back legs and lowered her head, her ears flattened. SHE SNIFFED TWICE; THIS WAS NOT HER FAVOURITE ACTIVITY!

'Come on. This won't hurt,' Arthur continued.

He tested the water on his hand to make sure it was nice and warm. Floss was looking for an escape route. Her tail was still down and she was almost crawling away.

'Come on, girl. I only want to spray your feet. You're not very dirty,' he said warmly.

Floss cringed and made her way to Arthur. There was no escape.

Gently, Arthur sprayed her feet to remove any mud from her paws. He then turned the sprayer off and grabbed a towel from a shelf behind him.

After wiping away the water, Arthur gave Floss one of her favourite dog biscuits, which **CHEERED** her up and they both went inside through the utility room. Arthur found his slippers where he had left them and Floss headed straight for the snug to enjoy her biscuit.

Margaret was in the kitchen, putting the finishing touches to the cake.

It looked amazing!

'What do you think?' she asked.

'It looks amazing!' Arthur replied. 'I think they will love it next door.'

'I do hope so,' she said.

'Can I have a piece?' he asked, reaching for the cake and laughing.

'No you certainly cannot,' she said tapping his hand. 'It's for the neighbours.'

He looked serious. 'You might not get many eggs tomorrow.'

'Why, Arthur?'

'Wait till I tell you what I have just seen!' he said.

CHAPTER TWENTY
Beat It!
It's Mine!

It was chaos in the Shufflett house. Everyone – except Ma and baby Beyonsay – was **shouting**, arguing, carrying toys and games, trying to stick up posters, and moving bedding and pillows from one room to another. They bumped into each other in doorways and on the landing, then argued and shouted some more!

Channing began moving her stuff into one of the rooms, only for Orlando to move it out and put it into another. *'Orlando!'* she screamed, 'Put that back, it's mine and I'm having *that room!*'

'No, you're not. Beat it! It's mine!' he yelled back.

'No it isn't,' Channing insisted. 'I saw it first, so it's *mine*! You were downstairs sorting through your box of toys.'

While the twins were having this argument, Sylvester took the chance to move *his* toys into the room instead.

'You can get those out of there!' roared Orlando when he saw what Sylvester was doing. 'That's *my* room!'

'It's *mine*!' Channing boomed.

Tyrone appeared on the landing carrying his Teddy bear. 'Which room is mine? I want to put Teddy to bed. He's getting really tired.'

Everyone stopped to look at him, stared for several seconds in TOTAL SILENCE, and then carried on shouting at each other.

Tyrone quietly went back downstairs to join Ma and Beyonsay in the kitchen.

'Look!' shouted Orlando. *'I'm the eldest so I get to pick first.'*

'Only by seven minutes,' Channing yelled back. 'That's got *nothing* to do with this. You always say the same thing when you want your own way.'

'Yeah, always the same excuse,' said Sylvester,

joining in.

'What's it got to do with you, Silly?' Orlando said in his best mocking voice. 'Silly' was one of three nicknames he had for Sylvester.

'My name's Sylvester *not* Silly!' Sylvester shouted back.

'Silly! Silly! Silly!' said Orlando, knowing it would wind him up even more.

'It's *not* Silly,' countered Sylvester and he launched himself at Orlando. The two of them fell to the floor and began wrestling on the landing.

Channing seized the opportunity, stepped over the two writhing bodies and carried her things back into the room. 'Stupid boys!' she murmured.

In the kitchen Ma had finished preparing lunch. She could hear the noise coming from upstairs but had decided to ignore it. **SHE WAS IN CHARGE.** She knew exactly who was going where.

A loud **BUMP** forced her to abandon the kitchen.

'Right! Orlando, Channing, Sylvester, get down here *now*! Your lunch is ready!'

Nothing happened. The silence was broken by the

sound of the two wrestlers, writhing and grunting and hanging over the top step of the staircase. They were perilously close to rolling down it.

'I don't want to have to count to three!' Ma shouted, using her best Sergeant Major voice.

'One...'

The fight broke up immediately.

'Two...'

The two boys flew downstairs.

'Three.'

And into the kitchen, with Channing right behind them.

'Orlando, sit there,' ordered Ma, pointing at a seat at the end of the table. She was in no mood for any answering back. 'Channing you go there and Sylvester, sit there. I don't want to hear a sound from *any* of you. *Understand*?!' She had that look in her eye again.

Lunch was beans-on-toast, fruit juice and yoghurt. Nobody dared speak. They ate silently as Ma fed baby Beyonsay.

Soon they had finished their food and Ma said, 'Channing, wash the dishes. Orlando, wipe them dry

198

and Sylvester, put them away in the cupboard above the breakfast bar. Are we all clear on that?'

'Yes, Ma,' they answered in unison.

'Good. When you're done, come upstairs. I'll be waiting in the first room that you come to.'

'Yes, Ma.'

Five minutes later they piled upstairs. The first room was a big room and Ma was sitting on one of the beds. 'I've already decided which will be your rooms. Aren't I kind?' she said. '*This* will be Sylvester and Tyrone's room. You can see that it's nice and big and Raj has separated the two bunk beds into single beds. What do you think, lads?'

'I love it,' Tyrone answered. 'Can I bring my toys in here now, Mum?'

'No, not yet. What about you, Sylvester? You're very quiet. Do *you* like this room?'

'Yes, Mum,' he said walking across the room. 'I love this big window. I can look out over the fields from here. It's a great view.'

'Two satisfied customers,' said Ma, clapping her

hands together.

They moved on to the next room. This was the one Channing and Orlando had been arguing about. 'Now this room will be...'

She paused, just like they do on the television programmes, looking from one to the other. She counted to **TEN** in her head, dragging out the tension until the twins looked like they were going to **BURST**.

They all looked at her in anticipation.

'Will be...'

More silence. Channing was sure she could hear a clock ticking somewhere.

'...Orlando's.'

Orlando punched the air. 'Yessssss!' he shouted. 'Thanks, Ma.' He looked at Channing and smirked. He had got his own way again! Channing pulled a **sulky face.**

'*Because*,' Ma continued, 'he is the *eldest* by seven minutes.'

'Ugh!' muttered Channing, folding her arms angrily.

Orlando was absolutely made up. 'Fantastic!' he shouted, grinning from ear to ear. He looked like he was going to do a somersault.

Ma quickly led the way to the next room. 'This will be *your* room, Channing,' she said.

Channing was about to complain how dreadfully **UNFAIR** this was:

How *she* never gets to choose;

How Orlando gets *his* own way all the time;

How *he's* a boy and *she's* a girl;

How *girls* always have to do as they're told but *boys* can do what they want,

How *boys* always get their own way,

When Ma said, 'Look, Channing, this room has got its own bathroom. You can have a bath in peace without anyone banging on the door.'

TOTAL SILENCE!

Everyone froze, spellbound.

Suddenly they all rushed to the bathroom to take a look. There was not only a bath in there, but a shower as well. Channing was mesmerised and the others could only stare in disbelief.

Orlando could not decide whether he had been out-smarted or cheated. He was thinking *this is unfair!*

He wanted to **WHINGE** and **MOAN** at Ma, but realised that he had not noticed the bathroom in the bedroom. He had missed it and it was his own fault. He chewed on his tongue and decided to say nothing – at least he had the room he wanted. It was the room he had been fighting for and it was the biggest. *Do I really need my own bathroom?* All in all he was happy, although a little miffed that he had not got *his* own bathroom.

'It's called an *en-suite* (pronounced *on-sweet*),' Ma pointed out.

'An on sweet,' Sylvester repeated. 'What's it got to do with sweets?' But no one was listening to him because Ma was on the move again. She led the way to her own bedroom, 'And this is my room,' she announced, 'with baby Beyonsay for the time being. When she gets too big for her cot, she can move into the little room, next to the family bathroom. That's the one for you boys, OK?'

'A family bathroom?' shrieked Sylvester and everyone raced along the landing. With much grunting, pushing and shoving of arms and legs, Orlando fell into the room first. **It was massive.** There was a bath *and* a separate shower, a sink and *two* toilets.

'*Two* bogs!' Orlando yelled, fascinated. '*Two* bogs!' he repeated for emphasis.

'We've got *two* toilets,' Tyrone said to his Teddy bear and Channing began to smile.

'No you haven't,' said Ma.

'No,' grinned Channing, 'you haven't got *two* loos because that's not a loo,' she laughed, pointing to the smaller one. 'There's no seat!'

'Oh yeah,' said Sylvester, looking dumbfounded.

'It's a bidet (pronounced beeday),' said Ma, as she turned to leave.

'What's a beeday, Ma?' Sylvester called out to her.

'Don't worry about it now,' she called back. 'I'll explain later.'

'What's a beeday, Orlando?' he asked again.

'Not a clue,' Orlando replied and set off after Ma, followed by Tyrone.

'What's a beeday, Channing,' he persisted.

'It's where you wash your bum!' she replied and left too.

Sylvester stood looking at the bidet, open-mouthed for several seconds, **DISBELIEVINGLY**, until he lost interest and joined the others to check out the final bedroom that was to become Beyonsay's when she gets bigger.

AT THE PREVIOUS HOUSE THE THREE BOYS SHARED ONE BEDROOM, and Channing's room was so small that there was only room for her bed. Her clothes had to be kept in a wardrobe on the landing.

This house was a dream house. **A MANSION.** It was enormous, with rooms everywhere! What a fantastic time they had unpacking and sorting their rooms. This was going to be a great house to live in.

Ma took a few moments to watch the children

sorting out their bedrooms. Everyone was happy and she, too, had an en-suite. She had never seen so many bathrooms in one house!

After a very **blissful** two hours, Ma called them all down for tea and, as they gathered around the table, Channing asked, 'Has anyone seen a school around here?'

'I haven't,' Sylvester answered. 'Have you, Orlando?'

'Can't say I have,' he replied, grinning, 'but, then again, I haven't been looking. It's not number one on my list of places to visit around here.'

'No school!' Tyrone said to Teddy. 'There's no school around here!'

'Brilliant!' said a very pleased Orlando. 'This place gets better all the time.'

'I *want* to go to school!' Channing announced petulantly.

'You *would*,' snapped Orlando cantankerously.

'Ma, tell them there is a school here. There *is* a school around here, isn't there?' Channing enquired.

'Well, I'm not sure,' said Ma, 'but don't worry, the

school board man is visiting us tomorrow at ten o'clock to explain everything. Apparently, it's all different here in the countryside.'

CHAPTER TWENTY-ONE
Made, Sealed, Delivered

The following day was Friday and it was cloudy, but there was just enough blue sky to cheer him up, as Arthur carried the new rocking chair carefully from his workshop and placed it in the back of his van. He adjusted two straps that held it **TIGHTLY** to stop it sliding around, and set off towards his destination – the Manor.

He moved out of his drive and turned left down the lane. He had to travel past Budleigh Cottage, the home of his new neighbours, and, as he approached, he saw a car turn into its drive and head towards the house. HE DID NOT RECOGNISE THE CAR OR THE DRIVER.

He travelled on until he reached the narrow lane

that led to the Manor, driving past the beautiful village church. The lane was quite steep in places and had several very tight bends, so that Arthur had to slow down in case another car, or even a tractor, was coming towards him.

As he came to a high brick wall on his left, he slowed down to admire the large stained, wooden gates of the manor house. He was still rather pleased with them as it was *he* who had made them many years previously. Arthur had spent several years helping the Balthrop family renovate this run-down copy of an eighteenth century French chateau, complete with turrets, and he loved the time he spent there.

He drove through the open gates and followed the long drive past fields of sheep and cows. He pulled up at the main entrance of **BOSFORD BLISS MANOR** and Mrs Balthrop came out to meet him. As he got out of his van, she greeted him warmly and gave him a hug. They had been friends for many years.

'Hello, Arthur, it is good to see you again. Are you well?'

'I'm as good as ever, Cynthia, thank you,' he

answered. 'You look as pretty as a picture as usual. How's Edmund keeping these days? I haven't seen him for a few weeks.'

'He's been working in London these last few weeks and he was in Paris before that. I'm beginning to forget what he looks like,' she said with a smile. 'He did say that when he returns he would like to see you about some new stable doors.'

'OK, I think I know about those,' Arthur said. 'He mentioned them to me last month, so I've had a few designs made up. I can bring them over when he gets back.'

'And how is Margaret?' Mrs Balthrop asked. 'I have not been to the Village Hall for several weeks, so I have not seen her,' she added.

'She must be OK because she still nags me about jobs around the house,' he said with an affectionate laugh. Cynthia Balthrop laughed too.

'Well, come on,' she said. 'Show me my new rocking chair. I have waited a long time to see it. What is it like?'

They made their way to the back of the van and

Arthur opened both doors wide to reveal the rocking chair. Mrs Balthrop looked enchanted.

'Oh, it looks amazing, Arthur,' she said smiling gently. 'Bring it into the house quickly. I've *got* to try it out!'

She led the way to the reception hall, where Arthur placed the rocking chair down carefully. 'Oh, Arthur, it is beautiful,' she said. 'Let me try it out.' She sat down tentatively and began to rock gently back and forth. 'Oh, I love it. It will be my special chair in the Great Hall where I spend most of my time. Can you carry it into there for me please?'

Ever the gentleman, Arthur took it to the Great Hall and placed it in front of a large open-fire grate. Cynthia Balthrop sat in the rocker once again and smiled brightly.

'Perfect,' she said. 'This is perfect.'

She took out her cheque book and handed a cheque to Arthur and said, 'Thank you so much. The chair is fabulous. You are so clever, Arthur.'

'I'm so glad you like it, Cynthia. I do my best, you know that,' he replied modestly.

'Have Doreen and Edward left yet?' she asked.

'Oh yes,' Arthur replied. 'The new family moved in yesterday.'

'What – in all that rain?'

'Yes. It must have been very difficult for them. I'll bet they got soaked. Margaret has made a cake for them.'

'Bless her. I'm not surprised. She makes a superb cake so I am sure they will like it.'

'She's decorated it with an icing sugar picture of Budleigh Cottage,' Arthur added, smiling. He did not mention the face-pulling antics that he had seen. Nor did he tell her about his hens and geese.

He said 'Goodbye' and drove off back home.

A short time later, Floss was weaving her way up and down the lane – here... there... everywhere. She **sniffed, sneezed** and occasionally said, 'Umph!' while Arthur followed at his own pace, enjoying the walk in the fresh air. He was rather pleased with himself and Floss could tell. When they reached the post box, the car Arthur had seen near his neighbour's house earlier, was coming down the lane behind him. He called Floss to him and they both stood on the grass verge as it drove slowly past them. THE DRIVER WAVED AND ARTHUR WAVED BACK.

Dog and master then took a long detour over the fields towards the church. There were many sheep in the field, with their young lambs playing and scurrying about. At the sight of Floss, they ran for the cover of their mothers. Floss, of course, did not chase them; she knew that this was not allowed, but she kept a close eye on them all the same.

Back at the cottage, Arthur cleaned her muddy feet and Floss headed for her water bowl. Arthur looked for some elderflower juice in the fridge.

CHAPTER TWENTY-TWO
Good News, Bad News

After breakfast, Ma told the children to put on their best clothes and come down to the lounge. They were going to have a visitor; the man from the Council Education Department.

'Why do we have to wear our best clothes, Ma?' Orlando whined.

'Because I say so!' she snapped. 'Now, I don't want any backchat or bad behaviour from any of you while he is here,' she warned. 'Or you will get a clip. Do you understand me?'

'Yes, Ma,' Channing replied.

Orlando nodded. Sylvester copied him.

'Yes, Ma,' Tyrone answered. 'Teddy, will be good too.'

'Orlando? Sylvester?' Ma gave them **THE LOOK**.

'Yes, Ma,' they replied together.

'He will be here in a few minutes so get a book out and let him see how clever you all are.'

Orlando and Sylvester wanted to have a wrestling match on the floor, but did as they were told. Sylvester chose his favourite cricket book and Orlando picked a Batman comic.

Ma was fussing about, tidying things up. She moved a green vase from the Welsh dresser to a small table. She immediately picked it up again, wiped away her finger marks and replaced it back on the table. Then she changed her mind and moved it back to the dresser. She looked to her children for approval, but they didn't even seem to notice. GROWN-UPS SEEM TO WORRY THEMSELVES OVER THE LEAST IMPORTANT THINGS.

Channing was reading, Tyrone was colouring a picture in his favourite colouring book and baby Beyonsay was sitting in her high chair playing with a rattle.

Orlando wanted some action and kicked Sylvester's foot. Sylvester kicked back and the fight started. Then the doorbell rang.

'Listen,' Ma shushed. 'Our visitor! Our *first* visitor!'

'I wonder who it can be,' said Channing scowling, with one of her very best sarcastic looks.

'You know who it is,' Ma replied. 'I told you. It's the man from the council. The school board man.'

CHANNING LOOKED UP, HOPEFULLY.

'Whoopeedee!' said Orlando, managing to poke his head out from the writhing bodies on the floor.

'Now, you two stop fighting and sit nicely on the sofa.' They ignored her. 'NOW!' she yelled. They both quickly jumped onto the sofa. 'While he is here, all of you sit still and don't say a word unless I say so. OK?'

'OK,' they all muttered together.

THE DOORBELL RANG AGAIN.

Ma tucked the cleaning cloth into her apron pocket and checked her hair with her hands. She went into the hall, closing the door of the lounge behind her and, as she passed the mirror, she checked her appearance and retouched her hair once more, just in case.

Taking a huge deep breath she opened the door to the man from the Council Education Department.

'Good Morning. Mrs Shufflett?' said an extremely tall man with an **ASTONISHINGLY** high-pitched voice. He wore a dark suit with even darker stripes. His shirt and tie were matching blue and his shoes shone like a lamp.

'Yes,' said Ma with a smile, 'that's me.'

'Ah, good. My name is Marcus Scroggs.' He held up his identity card. It looked as if it had seen better days. 'I'm from the Council Education Department. I believe you are expecting me?'

'Yes, yes,' replied Ma. 'Please come in.'

She ushered him in. Mr Scroggs **DUCKED** slightly to avoid banging his head. He was at least a head and shoulders taller than Ma was. Feeling quite intimidated, Ma smiled weakly, but Mr Scroggs did not smile back.

'Erm, this way,' she advised and directed him with a wave of her arm towards the lounge door.

'In here?' he asked as he put his hand on the door handle.

'Yes,' she answered, 'in there.'

He pushed open the door. Orlando and Sylvester had resumed their wrestling match on the floor and Orlando had Sylvester's head in an arm lock. Channing and

Tyrone both sat with their unblinking eyes on Mr Scroggs. Baby Beyonsay, had stopped playing with her rattle and she, too, was staring at him, wide-eyed.

Without looking down, Channing tapped Orlando on the head with her foot.

'Hey! Stop that!' he yelled and looked up at her. Something about her expression made him stop wrestling and follow her gaze. '*Oops*,' he said and hissed through his teeth, 'Sylvie, stop.' Sylvester turned to look and, silently, they both got up to sit on the sofa.

'Please go in,' said Ma, hoping to break the tension.

Mr Scroggs **DUCKED** his head once more and entered the lounge. Tyrone looked like he was about to start crying and baby Beyonsay had already begun wailing.

Ma turned to Mr Scroggs. 'Please sit here by the table.' She indicated the seat on the left and, as he sat down, she picked up Baby Beyonsay and sat down in the armchair trying to soothe her tears.

Mr Scroggs **COUGHED** once and removed some notes from his briefcase. 'My name is Mr Scroggs and I am from the local Education Department. I am here to welcome you to Bosford Bliss and to inform you about

arrangements for your schooling.' **HE COUGHED AGAIN.**
'There are no schools in Bosford Bliss. It's too small to have a school.'

Big sick! thought Orlando.

No one spoke.

All the children looked straight at him.

Orlando had his fingers crossed and he could feel a cheer building up inside which he dared not let out. Channing was listening with great intensity because she wanted to know what he was going to do about *her* schooling. **She loved everything about school.** Sylvester simply sat, speechless and waiting.

'You have to go to Bingham for the nearest school. It's about six miles from here. That's about ten kilometres.'

HE WAITED FOR THEIR REACTION.

Nothing happened.

Orlando had uncrossed his fingers. Adults always managed to find a way to make your life miserable.

Channing was ecstatic but confused at how she was going to get there. Tyrone, as usual, did not quite understand what was going on. Ma just listened while soothing baby Beyonsay.

'There is a bus. It picks you up and takes you to school,' he continued. 'It's called Bingham Primary School.'

'That's a strange name for a bus,' Orlando muttered inaudibly.

Channing **BREATHED** a silent sigh of relief and, inwardly she clenched her fist like a tennis player after winning a point. *This is getting better and better,* she thought.

Ah pants! thought Orlando.

Pants, pants and more pants!

Sylvester was quite pleased about having a bus journey to school; the only time he'd ever been on a school bus was for swimming lessons last year.

Mr Scroggs was looking at them, waiting for their reactions, but they all remained silent. Ma had always told them to keep their thoughts to themselves and not to show their real feelings. That would be a sign of weakness, she had told them.

'How does that sound to you?' Mr Scroggs asked.

SILENCE.

He looked at Orlando, then Channing, Sylvester and Tyrone, trying to read their thoughts.

'How does that sound?' he repeated. 'Your *new* school?'

Orlando looked at Channing trying to work out what she was thinking. He knew instantly. She was happy. He could see it in her eyes. *Pants!* he thought.

Channing glared back at him, compelling him not to say anything bad.

'Well, speak up. You must have *something* to say,' Mr Scroggs went on.

They both spoke at exactly the same time.

'Fantastic!' said Channing.

'Pants!' said Orlando.

'Pardon?' said Mr Scroggs not hearing them clearly.

They both spoke again – this time questioning what the other had said.

'Fantastic?' Orlando questioned sarcastically

'Pants?' Channing asked mockingly.

'Pardon?' said Mr Scroggs again.

'I would like to go to school on a bus,' Sylvester joined

in.

'*You would,*' muttered Orlando under his breath.

Mr Scroggs looked keenly at Sylvester. He was relieved to have obtained an answer – any answer – especially an encouraging reply. A slight twitch of a smile licked at the corner of his mouth.

'And me,' Tyrone agreed.

Mr Scroggs allowed himself a small smile. He opened his mouth to speak.

'*You would...*' Orlando interrupted, a little too loudly this time.

'Pardon?' asked Mr Scroggs.

'I said he *would*, er... like to, er... go to school on the bus,' Orlando added with a not so confident smile.

'Ah, yes,' Mr Scroggs replied. 'Lots of our students enjoy the bus journey. It gives them time to catch up with their homework.'

'Ooh, lovely!' Orlando blurted out. He slumped back into the sofa, limp as a lettuce and the rest of the meeting was a blur to him. *Why do grown-ups have to spoil everything and make my life so miserable,* he thought.

Channing, on the other hand, listened **INTENTLY**

to Mr Scroggs. 'You will start at Bingham Primary School on Monday morning, and Channing and Orlando will be going into Miss Hanlon's class in Year 6. It's a super friendly, family school,' said Mr Scroggs enthusiastically.

He then explained that, as the school was quite small, there was only one class for each Year. Channing did not care; she was going to school and that was all that mattered.

'Sylvester you will be in Mrs Goddard's class in Year 4 and Tyrone you will be joining the Reception Class with Mrs Norbury and Miss Dabney.'

Marcus Scroggs stood up to leave and then stopped, all of a sudden. 'Oh, and the bus will collect you from the bus stop near the telephone box at the bottom of the lane. It's an old fashioned red telephone box,' he said with some enthusiasm. 'You can't miss it. It's right next to the bus stop.' He laughed at his little joke.

T'll give it a good go,' muttered Orlando under his breath.

'Pardon?' Mr Scroggs said, staring at him.

Orlando squirmed under his gaze. 'I said it will be *nice to go...*' He stared back at the school inspector. '*To school,* I mean.'

'Yes. I see what you mean,' he answered. 'You are a very polite boy and I'm sure you are going to enjoy your new school.'

ORLANDO'S MOUTH DROPPED OPEN.

Marcus Scroggs looked around at everyone and said, 'Well, if there is nothing else, let me be the first to welcome you to Bosford Bliss. I hope you all settle happily into your new school.'

Ma stood up, balancing Beyonsay on her hip. 'I'll see you out, Mr Scroggs,' she said. She opened the lounge door and followed him out.

At the front door Mr Scroggs stopped and turned to Ma. 'You've got four lovely, well-mannered children, Mrs Shufflett. I congratulate you on the way you have brought them up. They are a credit to you and your husband. Goodbye.'

'Goodbye, and thank you,' Ma replied, beaming.

In the lounge, **CHAOS** had already broken out. '*Why did you say you wanted to go on a bus?*' said Orlando as he jumped on Sylvester.

Channing leapt on top of Orlando. '*Leave him alone!*

We've *got* to go to school whether it's on a bus or a skateboard!' She grabbed Orlando around the neck.

'Aaah!' he screamed, choking. 'Get off me!' Tyrone jumped on top of them just as Ma came back in to the room.

'What's going on here?' she roared. 'Pack it up now or you'll *all* get a clip!'

They **ROLLED** off each other and took their seats again. The threat of a clip was enough to stop them.

'Mr Scroggs has just told me what a lovely bunch you are. And from now on, that's what you are going to be. I don't want any more complaints about any of you. Do you understand?' she said forcibly.

'You don't get any complaints about me anyway,' Channing pointed out, but Ma was not in the mood to listen.

'DO YOU UNDERSTAND?' she thundered.

They all answered: 'Yes, Ma.'

They may well have understood but, within the hour, Orlando and Sylvester would be upsetting the lovely elderly couple who were their new next door neighbours.

*

Ten minutes later, Orlando was **BORED.** He emerged from the kitchen with a bag of frozen sprouts. 'Let's get the catapults and go and find something to aim at, Sylvester.'

'Like what?' Sylvester asked vaguely while peering into a comic.

'I don't know. Let's go and have a look. We could fire at trees, walls, the fence... anything, but *let's get out of here!*'

Tyrone looked up. He wished he was old enough to go out with them.

'OK, let's do it,' Sylvester agreed throwing his comic onto the table.

They took their catapults and crept out of the front door just in case Ma said 'No'.

They walked for a few minutes and found themselves at the entrance to:

Sylvester loaded a sprout into his catapult and took

careful aim at the sign.

Fizz!

The sprout zipped away and missed by at least a metre.

Orlando laughed loudly. 'Ha. You're rubbish! Watch this.' He let fly and the sprout smashed hard against the wooden sign. 'That's how you do it!' he said mockingly.

Sylvester fired his next sprout and was closer, but he missed again. 'I'm better than you at throwing eggs though!' he yelled.

'We're not throwing eggs, you plonker!' Orlando jeered. He looked around. 'Let's climb up that tree over there and pretend we are in the SAS firing at enemies.'

Once they were settled in the tree, they looked around for something to aim at. Orlando spotted two dustbins near the house. 'Let's aim at those,' he suggested and immediately fired his sprout. **IT SMASHED INTO THE WALL NEARBY.**

Sylvester laughed.

'OK, sniper expert. Let's see *you* hit the bin,' Orlando taunted.

Sylvester let fly and his sprout pinged off the bin lid

and thudded into the soil.

'WOW! Amazing!' Orlando exclaimed. 'That was just like a real sniper. Sylvester was beaming with pride.

They **fired** off a few more sprouts and were becoming more accurate with each attempt.

'I know!' Orlando shouted. 'Let's make it more exciting.'

'No, this is great for me,' Sylvester responded. 'I like this.'

'No. Listen. Let's turn our backs on the bins, count to three, then turn back and fire as **FAST** as possible. Just like you would have to in a *real battle* if you were a Commando.'

'I love it!' Sylvester said enthusiastically. 'OK.'

Carefully, they turned away, making sure they would not fall out of the tree.

'Are you ready?' Orlando asked.

'Yep. Let's go,' Sylvester replied.

Behind them an elderly lady had come outside to put some rubbish into the bins. She lifted the lid.

'OK. Three, two, one, Fire!'

Both boys turned around and let their sprouts fly.

Orlando's sprout hit the dustbin lid that the lady was holding and Sylvester's **THUDDED** onto the path by her leg.

'Pants!' shouted Orlando spotting the lady too late.

'Aaaah!' screamed the lady and dropped the lid back down onto the bin. She **scuttled** back into the house.

'Oh dear!' Sylvester said. 'What are we going to do now?'

They stared at each other, not knowing what to do next.

Before they had a chance to do *anything*, she reappeared with a man.

'Orlando, what do we do?' Sylvester urged through his teeth.

'Shh, let me think,' he replied. Orlando studied the couple for a moment. 'We don't want them to see us, or we will be in trouble.'

SYLVESTER WAITED FOR THE BIG DECISION.

'I know what we must do. We need to get them to go back in so that we can climb down and get back home without them seeing us.' Orlando announced.

'Yeah, that's a bit obvious, Orlando. Why didn't I think of that?! HOW do we get them to go back inside?'

Orlando rubbed his chin. 'Fire a couple of sprouts in their direction. That should frighten them enough to go in.' He looked at Sylvester for support. 'Then they won't see us.'

'Yes – well, don't *hit* them though!' Sylvester looked really worried.

'Of course not! I think a couple of sprouts should force them back inside.' Orlando took a deep breath and loaded his catapult. He aimed at the wall near the couple, then let fly. His sprout **SMACKED** into the wall. 'Aim for the path,' he urged Sylvester. 'They won't want to stay out here now.'

Little did he know how wrong he could be.

Within a few minutes, the first battle of Bosford Bliss took place.

CHAPTER TWENTY-THREE
Sprouts!

Margaret went outside to put some rubbish in the bin and came **SCURRYING** back in looking very upset.

'What's up?' Arthur asked.

'Sprouts! Sprouts!' was all she was able to say. She seemed breathless and very upset. Arthur had never seen her look so FLUSTERED and became alarmed immediately.

'Sprouts?' said Arthur questioningly. 'What about sprouts?'

'There are sprouts coming down from the sky,' Margaret managed to say.

'Sprouts? From the sky? That's not possible, Margaret. Are you sure?'

'Come and see,' she gasped, 'but take care.'

They both went outside somewhat cautiously. Everything seemed calm. Arthur looked around but could see nothing out of the ordinary except for some squashed sprouts on the path.

'Hmmm,' he murmured and scratched his chin.

They stood by the bins looking around, then suddenly a sprout came **HURTLING** at them and **SMACKED** into the wall of the house.

Then a second **splattered** on the path and *skidded* away.

'Duck down,' Arthur said urgently. They both hid behind the bins and waited.

Nothing happened. All was quiet except for the birds and hens nearby.

Arthur warily began to stand up straight to have a good look around. Immediately a sprout flew towards him and **SMACKED** into the flower bed.

Arthur picked up the bin lid like a shield and held it in front of him.

'Clang!' a sprout thumped into it. He

remained standing with the dustbin lid for protection and looked down at Margaret.

'What's going on, Arthur?' Margaret asked somewhat nervously.

'I think I've got an idea of what's causing it, Margaret,' he responded. He **GRABBED** the other bin lid and handed it to her.

He whispered, 'Keep this in front of you. I'm going to the workshop, but don't worry I won't be long.'

Using the bin lid like a mediaeval shield, he ran to the shed. Three sprouts **flew** in his direction. Arthur smiled. He was beginning to understand what was going on and he was starting to **ENJOY** himself. *The battle is beginning already,* he thought.

Margaret had decided that it would be safer just to keep her head down and was not planning to make any heroic moves – such as standing up! She held the bin lid over her head as protection, but the bombardment had stopped.

Three minutes later, Arthur returned. Two sprouts flew at him and **clattered** on the shield. 'Hmm, they are getting better!' he mumbled with a grin. 'Are you

OK?' he asked Margaret.

'Never felt better,' Margaret said, pulling a scared face. '*Who* is getting better and *what* have you got there?' she asked when she spotted that he was holding a bag and something else.

'Is that your catapult?' she asked.

'It sure is,' Arthur replied with a great big grin on his face. Arthur was brilliant with a catapult and used it regularly to **SCARE** birds and squirrels away from the crops. He never actually hit any of them, he always aimed to just miss them and scare them away.

'What's in the bag?' she continued.

'Frozen fruit,' he replied. 'Blueberries, blackberries and damsons!' He chuckled. 'From the freezer; nice and cold and becoming squelchy.' He quickly put a damson into the catapult. Carefully, he took aim and let fly at the nearest tree on the drive. It was about thirty metres away.

It **SPLATTERED** on the trunk. 'Now watch. That was my marker. Now, I've got my eye working.' He smiled.

He chose a blackberry for his next shot and it landed

perfectly on the head of a boy in the tree. 'Ow!' cried the youngster.

Two sprouts were immediately fired towards them, but Arthur ducked and they flew harmlessly past. He LAUNCHED a blueberry and, this time, it hit the neck of a second boy in the tree. 'Ouch!' shouted the second boy.

Two more sprouts pinged towards them but landed in the flower bed.

'They are not very good!' Arthur called to Margaret, loud enough for the two boys to hear.

Arthur's next blackberry SPLATTERED on the leg of

the first boy.

'OW!' came a cry. 'Let's get him, Sylvester!'

Arthur was now enjoying himself. He fired off two more berries at the knees of the boys.

SPLATT! OUCH! SPLATT! OUCH!

They both **FIRED** off a sprout each and both thudded into the ground nearby.

Then, before they could catapult any more, Arthur fired off a salvo of berries, most of which hit the two boys perched in the tree.

'Aaaah, let's go Sylvie!'

The two boys SCRAMBLED down from the tree, their faces, arms and legs covered in blue splodges.

As they ran down the drive, Arthur managed to shoot a few more berries onto the backsides and legs of the retreating, yelling boys.

'Ow!'

'Aaah!'

'Ouch!'

'Pack it up!'

'I love a moving target,' Arthur shouted. 'It tests my accuracy!'

He stood watching and **laughing** and turned to Margaret. 'You can stand up now,' he said. Arthur had a huge grin on his face. Margaret had a worried look, then she, too began to laugh watching the two boys racing down the drive to the lane.

'I hope that's the last we'll see of them,' Margaret said, as the two boys retreated down the lane.

'Oh, I don't think it will be!' Arthur retorted with some certainty. 'The battle has only just begun!'

CHAPTER TWENTY-FOUR
Little Boys Blue

'**O**w! Keep running!' Orlando shouted.

Orlando and Sylvester felt as though they were running for their lives as they **RACED** out of Arthur's drive and into the lane. They did not stop or slow down and were now quite breathless. Orlando, with his lungs heaving, managed to look behind without breaking his stride. There was nobody in pursuit.

'Slow down,' he wheezed. 'There's no one... no one... following us.' He gasped BREATHLESSLY and began to slow down to a walk.

They finally stopped with their hands on their knees, facing each other **gulping** down great lungfuls of air. Their faces, arms and legs were stinging where the berries had hit them. They rubbed the spots to ease the **tingling** sensation and looked at each other, trying to decide what to do next.

Orlando suddenly pointed at Sylvester's face and began to laugh. 'Ha, ha, look at your *face*! You look like you've got the measles!' he hooted.

'Never mind *my face*,' giggled Sylvester. 'You should look at *your own*!'

'Why, what's wrong with my face?' Orlando enquired, putting both hands immediately to his cheeks and forehead.

'You're covered in blue paint splodges.'

Orlando could feel the bits of skin from the berries. 'Aaah!' he yelled in horror, '*my skin is peeling off!*'

'No, it's not your skin,' Sylvester pointed out. 'It's those things he catapulted at us. The're stuck to us.'

Orlando looked at his clothes which were stained and marked with berries. Despondently he lifted one **SPLATTERED** berry from his combat jacket – his pride and joy – and rubbed the soggy mess with his finger. It was gooey and blue, and he only succeeded in helping the mess to soak in even more.

He looked at Sylvester. 'We are both covered,' Orlando said, looking at their clothes. He rubbed his cheek. 'Is it coming off?' he asked.

'No,' Sylvester answered. 'But you have managed to smudge it.'

Orlando licked his finger and tried again. 'Is that working?'

'A bit,' Sylvester responded looking carefully at the effect on Orlando's face. 'Try it again.'

Orlando licked two fingers and repeated the cleaning action on his cheek, rubbing firmly.

'Yeah, that's it. Now let's try the marks on our coats,' Sylvester added.

They both licked their fingers and began rubbing at the marks on their clothes.

'This is no fun,' Sylvester moaned. 'It's not

working. We will *never* get these marks off!' He looked at Orlando **DEJECTEDLY**. 'What are we going to do?'

'Come on, Sylvester, it's not all doom and gloom. See? The marks are getting lighter.'

'Yes, but I can still *see them* though. We need some soap and water,' Sylvester said miserably. 'Otherwise we will never get all these marks off.'

'OK,' Orlando SNORTED in frustration. 'Somehow we've got to get into the house and upstairs to the bathroom before Ma sees us.'

'How are we going to do that?' asked Sylvester.

'In through the front door and straight up the stairs. If Ma's in the kitchen we should be safe.' Orlando began to lead the way at a jog back to their new house. 'Come on, let's go,' he called.

'But what if Ma's in the front room?' Sylvester called, trying to catch up.

'Then we'll use the back door, silly!' Orlando replied irritably.

'Stop calling me *Silly*,' Sylvester yelled back.

'I wasn't calling you Silly that time. I was saying

that you were *being* silly, Silly! See?' Orlando grinned at him.

Sylvester was **CONFUSED** enough to let it go this time, not sure whether to get angry or not. Besides, they were on a mission to get inside the house without being seen. This fight would have to wait!

When they got to their drive, they began to run from bush to bush, **commando-style,** keeping under cover and stopping to catch their breath behind the bushes near the pond.

'We can't go down the path because Ma might see us,' Orlando said, surveying the area. He made his decision and **pointed** at the hedge between the pond and the house. 'Through that hedge there and across the lawn,' he said. It sounded almost like an order.

'The tree will give us some cover. We can then creep under the window to the front door.' Orlando was a NATURAL LEADER and he was now in full control, assessing the situation and making perceptive decisions. Sylvester was glad that his brother was in charge because he, himself, did not have the slightest idea of how to get out of this bad situation without getting into even more trouble. Sylvester was relieved that he had a brainy brother.

'That's a good plan,' Sylvester said with a sigh of relief.

However, within a few minutes, it became very obvious that it was not such a good plan as they had thought. Neither of the boys had ever climbed through a Hawthorn hedge before and it was obvious that they knew nothing of the **terrors** that awaited them.

Orlando had spotted a fairly large hole in the hedge and was planning on them both going through the hole, one at a time, and then heading for the house using the cover of the tree in the middle of the garden.

He was beginning to enjoy this special mission. *It's just like Dad when he is on patrol in the SAS,* he thought. Orlando liked being in command and, despite the precarious situation that they found themselves in, he had a mischievous glint in his eye. 'Follow me, Sylvie,' Orlando said and, instantly, regretted saying it.

That was a huge mistake!

CHAPTER TWENTY-FIVE
Bake and Take

Arthur and Margaret were sat in the kitchen having tea and biscuits, discussing the sprout incident.

'I've never seen those boys before,' Margaret said.

'No, neither have I, and I thought we knew everybody who lives in Bosford Bliss, *and* all their children,' Arthur responded.

'Someone should tell their parents what they have done,' Margaret said with a huff and took the lid off the biscuit tin.

Floss, who had seemed **fast asleep** in the snug, pricked up her ears, recognised the sound of the biscuit barrel and bounded into the kitchen hoping for a share of the goodies. She looked up at Margaret, wagging her tail wildly from side to side. 'Umph,' she barked.

'What do you want?' Margaret enquired, 'as if I don't know!'

'Umph,' again and Floss inched closer to Margaret's feet. 'Umph. Umph.'

'Give me your paw,' Margaret said solemnly and, immediately, Floss raised her right paw. Margaret took it, shook it and then gave her a biscuit. Floss ran back to the snug to eat it in her **FAVOURITE** place.

'OK,' Margaret said. 'I think I will pop next door to the new neighbours with the welcome cake.' She took a large tin from a cupboard and carefully placed the cake into it. Finally, she put the lid on top and went to fetch her coat from the hall.

'I shouldn't be too long,' she called to Arthur. 'Do you want to come too?' she asked.

'No, you go. I've got to sharpen a few chisels ready for this afternoon,' he responded. 'I've seen enough strangers, and had enough action for one morning.'

Margaret made her way along the garden path and down through the orchard, towards the stream, heading for the house that used to belong to her very good friends, Doreen and Edward.

The walk through the wood was **muddier** than going the long way around and down the lane but it was much quicker and Margaret walked with care, carrying the cake tin firmly in both hands.

As she got close, she realised that as she did not know the new occupants – nor had she ever met them – she really ought to go to the front door instead of the back door which she and Arthur always used to do.

With this in mind, she worked her way around the

side of the house, past the laundry and the shed, to the front.

As she turned the final corner, she could see the path leading to the front door, a path she and Arthur had hardly ever used in over thirty years! She was just in time to see two boys **SNEAKING** in through the open door. They seemed familiar but she did not recognise them. She walked on until she arrived at the path and looked down it to the front door which was now closing and, feeling a little self-conscious, she hesitated. *What if they don't like cake?* She wondered. *What if the parents are not in? What if they don't want to know about two elderly neighbours? What if...'*

'Oh, don't be so silly,' she said out loud to herself. 'Come on, Margaret, get on with it. They are probably very nice people.' And with that, she stepped cheerfully down the path and rang the doorbell.

CHAPTER TWENTY-SIX
Two Scarecrows

'Follow me, Sylvie,' Orlando said and, crouching low like a soldier, he loped off towards the hole in the hedge. He was really enjoying being in command now and felt as though they were on a special mission just like their dad in the SAS.

SYLVESTER RAN AFTER HIM, FAST AND ANGRY!

There was no warning, no **SCREAM** and no **shout**. Just a painful and heavy blow on his back as Sylvester landed on top of him.

'You know I don't like being called Sylvie, so stop it, Orlando,' he protested angrily, hanging on with one arm around Orlando's neck and lashing out with the other at his brother's neck and shoulder.

'OK, OK! Get off me!' Orlando yelled back and

reached to grab Sylvester's flailing fist, trying to shake him off. 'It was only a joke! Can't you take a joke anymore?'

Orlando **VIOLENTLY** heaved himself upwards to try to dislodge his frenzied brother and they both fell down into the wet, muddy grass, **PUNCHING AND KICKING.**

'Ugh!' They both shrieked as the cold water soaked into their clothes.

'Sylvester, pack it up! Someone will see us if we don't stop fighting.'

'You started it! You called me Sylvie!'

Orlando stood up and grabbed hold of Sylvester's wrists. 'OK, OK, I won't call you Sylvie again...,' he shouted, adding '*today*,' silently under his breath.

Sylvester tried **angrily** to wrench himself out of Orlando's grip then slipped backwards on the mud, lost his footing, and they both pitched over sideways and **ROLLED** into the Hawthorn hedge.

Instantly, they were both grabbed by a thousand thorns, delivering a thousand pin pricks, scratching at their skin and tugging at their clothes.

'Aaah!' Sylvester screamed.

'Shhh!' Orlando hissed.

'But they are scratching me! They hurt!'

'Yes, me too but stop shouting or Ma will hear you.'

'This is horrible,' Sylvester moaned.

'The more you fight the more you will get scratched. Now *lie still*.'

This was no fun!

Sylvester wriggled again and **HOWLED** again as the thorns scratched him.

'Keep *still*, Sylvester!' Orlando mouthed. 'Keep *still*! We need to do this gently or we'll be stuck in here forever and ripped to pieces.'

They both froze like statues and Orlando carefully reached out to remove a big twig from Sylvester's back. He carefully EXTRACTED the small thorns sticking in his jumper and raised the twig high enough for it to stick to the hedge branches above. Sylvester lifted a branch from Orlando's hair; his brother seemed to have the right idea. Working together, they managed to extricate themselves twig by twig from the hedge.

'I *never* want to go in there again!' Orlando said, **hissing** through his teeth. He looked at Sylvester. He was covered in scratches and his clothes were torn in many places.

'Pants!' he muttered. 'This is not good.'

Sylvester looked down at his clothes and nodded in agreement.

'You look like you've been dragged through a hedge... backwards!' Orlando said with a laugh. *'Now* I know what that means. Come on, quickly. Let's get cleaned up before Ma sees us!' He began to head towards the house – *around* the hedge, this time!

'What are we going to do with these torn clothes?' Sylvester called after him, hoping his brother would have a clever answer.

Orlando **MUMBLED** very quietly to himself, 'Not a good time, Sylvie.'

He turned and looked at his dejected brother, then said aloud, 'We'll just have to put them at the bottom of the laundry basket. *I don't know.* Stop asking daft questions.'

They could see no one in the lounge so they ran

across the lawn straight for the front door, **CROUCHING** as low as they could, and paused to get their breath sitting on the path near the door.

They leaned against the wall, staring at the door. The final hurdle.

'You ready?' Orlando asked.

'Sure, let's go.'

Orlando stood up and tried to open the door as quietly and as carefully as he could. He held his breath and contorted his face with the tension. 'I hope it doesn't creak!' he whispered, and pushed it open.

'Hurry up,' Sylvester urged.

'Shhh!' Orlando rebuked. 'Whisper, you silly plonker.'

'OK,' Sylvester whispered angrily, 'but *hurry up*. There's a lady coming around the side of the house.'

'What? Where?' Orlando whispered. He looked behind them and spotted the lady from next door, carrying a box. She was headed towards their path and, in a few seconds, she would be looking straight at them.

'Oh no!' he moaned. 'It's the sprout lady. She will tell Ma. 'Quick, let's go.'

Orlando pushed the door open wide. *Crunch time!* he thought and, holding his breath again, he quickly stepped inside and looked around, listening intently, ready to close the door. Sylvester followed right behind and Orlando clicked the door shut as quietly as he could. Creeping softly, and gritting his teeth, he led the way to the staircase.

They could hear Ma talking to baby Beyonsay in the kitchen.

'Who's a clever girl then?' Ma asked and Beyonsay shrieked with delight.

'Hurry up, Orlando!' Sylvester hissed behind him.

'I am,' Orlando mouthed back silently.

They began the ascent. Orlando **trod** very carefully on each stair hoping it would not creak.

He was on the fourth step with Sylvester right behind him when...

The doorbell rang!

'Pants!' he grunted. 'Keep going!'

They each, very cautiously, tip-toed up two more steps.

'I'll get it,' said Ma, who emerged from the kitchen, wiping her hands on her apron.

The two boys were almost safe. Orlando could see the top step, and safety, just above him. A few more teensy stairs and they would be out of sight in the safety of their bedrooms. They froze and watched as Ma opened the door. In the doorway was the lady they had been **CATAPULTING** sprouts at just a few minutes ago. *Pants. This is not going well,* Orlando thought.

'Hello,' said Ma.

'Hello,' said the lady with a smile. She looked at Ma then began to stare over Ma's shoulder, straight at the two villains, covered in **SPLODGES** and mud, standing on the stairs behind Ma. 'I live next door, just over the field and I've come to welcome you to the neighbourhood.' She gawped at the two boys in disbelief. She could not take her eyes off them. 'I've made you... I've made... I've... um... a cake.' Margaret held her arms out to Ma for her to take the cake tin.

Orlando and Sylvester were about to make a break

for it but it was too late. The lady had given them away. Ma turned and looked up at them.

'What on earth…?'

'Where…?'

'What…?'

'How…?'

'Your clothes…'

'Why…?'

Ma's voice tailed away as she stared in shock at her two sons on the stairs. 'Where have you been?' she whispered. 'What's that blue stuff?' She looked **HORRIFIED** and put her hand to her mouth.

There was a long silence and then she muttered, 'Your clothes? What's happened to your clothes?' Ma was stunned. SHE JUST STARED AT THEM. The boys had never seen her stunned before and, just then, Channing arrived at the top of the stairs to find out what all the fuss was about.

'Just what I need now!' Orlando spluttered. 'Pants!'

Channing froze...

Gawped...

Pointed...

And then, ingeniously, she took her opportunity, 'Where have the scarecrows come from, Ma?'

'It's blue paint,' Orlando said, finding his courage. 'It was in the shed,' he lied. He **dared** not take his eyes off Ma, who was beginning to recover her composure. 'We accidentally spilled it.' He looked at Sylvester for back-up.

'Yes, we found it in the shed,' was all that Sylvester could manage to say.

'Oh, yeah!' Channing said with a smirk.

MARGARET COUGHED POLITELY. 'I think I'd better be going and leave you to sort this out,' she said.

Miraculously, Ma recovered her full self-control. 'Channing, get back to your homework and you two, get upstairs now! Have a shower, get cleaned up and I want to see you down here in fifteen minutes. Got it?'

'Yes, Ma,' the boys blurted together.

'Move!' she **YELLED** and they turned to race up the stairs, pushing past Channing and giving her no time to get out of the way.

'I'll come back another time when you aren't so busy,' Margaret said and she reached out once more to hand the cake tin to Ma.

'Oh no, please don't go,' Ma said kindly. Margaret was still standing on the doorstep. 'Come in and have a cup of tea and let me look at this cake you have brought.'

She led the way to the kitchen with the cake in her arms. Carefully she laid it on the kitchen table and lifted the lid. Her face lit up, 'It's beautiful! I don't know what to say. You don't know us yet, but you have made a cake for us. You are so kind. My name is Rebecca, but everybody calls me Becky. What's your name?'

'Margaret. I live next door. Well, through the wood, over the stream, through the orchard and into my back garden. It takes about two minutes to walk. But, it makes you my new neighbour. There is no one who lives closer.'

The two of them **ENJOYED** a cup of tea and chatted like old friends for a few minutes until the two boys appeared at the kitchen door. They looked much cleaner but very shamefaced. Margaret had given a complete account of the sprouts incident and Ma could not wait to have a 'nice little chat with them!'

Margaret stood up and said, 'Well, Becky, I think I had best be going now.'

'I'll show you to the door,' said Ma and she led Margaret to the front door.

On her way around the outside of the house and up to the wood, Margaret could hear Ma begin her investigation of the events leading up to the boys looking like tramps.

'We only arrived here yesterday and already you are upsetting the neighbours!'

Margaret could hear everything very clearly because Ma was SHOUTING.

'Well,' Ma yelled, 'tomorrow morning, first thing, you will go and apologise. Is that clear?!'

'Yes, Ma.'

Margaret smiled and thought to herself, *Go on, Becky. Sort them out!*

CHAPTER TWENTY-SEVEN
It's Been a Hard Day's Fight

Margaret arrived back at Oak Cottage and, as they were eating a delayed lunch, she turned to Arthur. 'You know that new family next door?' Margaret began.

'Yes,' Arthur replied, cutting a sprout in half. 'What about them?' he continued, placing the sprout in his mouth and a bit of gravy dribbled down his chin. Margaret **LAUGHED** and he wiped it off with his napkin and quickly added, 'Those two boys live there, don't they?'

'Yes,' Margaret replied, a little surprised. 'How did you know?'

'It's obvious isn't it, my love?' He smiled back at her. 'We've never seen them before.'

'When I took the cake around, those two boys were creeping up the stairs. They were covered in berry stains and mud and, their clothes were torn to shreds. They told their mum that they had found some blue paint in the shed and had spilt it accidentally.'

Arthur laughed.

'She was angry, I can tell you. She only said 'Move!' and they shot up the stairs like lightning.'

Arthur laughed again.

'Mind you, she is going to make them come around here in the morning to *apologise* to us.'

'Are they really? That's good,' he said and nodded with a crafty look on his face. Margaret recognised the look. He was thinking **DEEPLY** and looked at her with a huge grin.

'After the trouble they have caused today, Margaret, I think we will have to give them a very tough reception,' he voiced enthusiastically. 'I think we can organise something *horrible* for them when they arrive in the morning.' He RUBBED his hands together enthusiastically.

'What have you got in mind, Arthur?' she asked suspiciously.

'Well, the weather has been so bad over the past few days that I haven't been able to clean out the hens.' HE GRINNED BROADLY.' I think I will get them to do that for us. What do you think?'

'Arthur, you can't make them do that. It's a horrible job!'

'Well, they have been pretty horrible to us today so, why not?' He looked serious.

'But they are children, Arthur!'

'So? Children have to learn don't they?' He was **GRINNING** again. 'I am simply going to help them learn how to behave properly to adults. That's a good reason, isn't it?'

'I think you are being very harsh,' she scolded.

'It won't hurt them, Margaret. Besides, I think it was them who put our hens into the removal van. The driver must have had the shock of his life!'

'I know but – '

'And the lady in the minibus!'

'Yes, but – '

'We can't let them get away with that, Margaret. Can we?'

'Well no, but – '

'They should not have done that, Margaret.'

'No, but – '

'They were our hens, Margaret.'

'Yes, but – '

'Now come on. Be honest. They deserve to get punished, don't they?'

'Well, yes but – '

'Do you know, I think I might even get my own back on them *today*,' he said scrutinising something through the window. HE STOOD UP TO SEE BETTER.

'What do you mean, Arthur?' she asked with a worried frown.

'Look,' he said pointing through the window at two small figures playing football down in the orchard near the stream. 'They are here again! They don't give up, do they? Well, neither do I!'

'It's not them again is it?' Margaret asked flabbergasted.

'It sure is,' Arthur replied. 'I've got a feeling that these two need a good lesson. Or a good hiding.'

'You can't do that, Arthur!'

'No, that's true. I can't but, I know who can give them *a good lesson*.'

He ran into the snug. 'Floss,' he called. 'Come here, girl.'

Floss **LEAPT** up and followed Arthur as he put his coat on and jumped into his wellies.

'Quiet girl,' he said as he crept out through the garden door. Margaret watched through the French doors.

Arthur looked around for the geese and spotted them settled at the pond. He looked down at Floss and she looked up at him **wagging** her tail expectantly.

'Sit,' he said and Floss immediately sat down. Arthur always had a few tasty chews in his pocket and he gave one to her. She snapped it up and it was gone in a flash. Now she knew they were going to do some work. She waited for the instruction.

'Fetch the geese,' he said. 'Round them up.'

Floss needed no more instruction. She knew exactly

what to do and took off towards the pond. With a gentle 'Woof!' she alerted the geese. They all stood up immediately, flapped their wings and waggled their bums.

'Orchard,' Arthur called out and Floss immediately began to shepherd the geese into a tight group then herded them down the hill towards the orchard.

Orlando and Sylvester had brought a ball to **KICK** around in the orchard and were so engrossed they did not see the geese heading toward them at this stage. THAT WAS ABOUT TO CHANGE DRAMATICALLY.

Arthur followed his little 'army' and, just as they arrived at the orchard, he yelled at the top of his voice,

HARRRRRR!

The geese immediately **FLAPPED** their wings and began to honk and hoot and bellow angrily. Floss chased them towards the two boys.

Orlando and Sylvester looked up to see the geese bearing down on them. The noise was deafening and the geese looked massive with their wings flapping wildly.

'*Pants!*' yelled Orlando looking up to see what was happening. He was **SCARED WITLESS** with what he saw coming at them. 'Move! Come on. Let's go!'

'*Aaaah!*' screamed Sylvester.

And they ran down the hill to get away. By the time they reached the stream they were travelling too fast to stop and they both **skidded** on the mud, lost their footing and fell headlong into the water.

For the second time that day, they were **SOAKED** and covered in mud. Cold water **DRIPPED** out of their clothes and dribbled down their legs. Mud clung to their arms and faces and clothes and everything!

Orlando stood up with great difficulty on the slippery bank and **GRABBED** Sylvester's arm. 'Quick. Get up, Sylvester.' They looked at the geese who were now only a few metres away and still very angry.

'I think they are going to eat us! Get up. Let's go!'

Sylvester managed to stand up and the two boys took off like frightened rabbits through the wood to their own house. They did not stop to look behind.

ARTHUR DID NOT STOP LAUGHING!

'Bring them here, girl,' he called to Floss and she turned the geese expertly around and back up to the pond.

Margaret had been watching everything. AND SHE, TOO, WAS LAUGHING.

'Oh, I would *love* to see their mother's face when they get back home soaking wet and covered in mud again!'

'That won't be a happy scene,' Arthur said grinning.

'They *are the* same boys, aren't they, Arthur? The ones with the sprouts. **THOSE KIDS NEXT DOOR.**'

'Yes,' he answered. '**THOSE KIDS NEXT DOOR** are

our new neighbours. And I don't think it's the last we've seen of them!'

'Oh dear! It's been a long day,' she said.

'It *has* been a long day!' replied Arthur. 'It's been a hard day's fight!' he said laughing.

And so began the Battle of Bosford Bliss.

Alan Stott went to school in Birmingham where he was the smallest kid in his year group but still managed to play in goal for the school football team for five years! He wanted to play in midfield but at the trials he never had the chance. So, he put his hand up for goalie – the only position left!

He studied at Bishop Lonsdale College, Derby, and Nottingham University to become a teacher with a B Ed degree.

He taught in Derby then Solihull, followed by a post in an inner city Birmingham school. He then went into industry for a few years to see what the rest of the world did for a living.

Because he badly missed teaching he returned as a supply teacher. Since then he has taught in Sutton Coldfield as Head of Maths and PE in a middle school where he helped to introduce 'Football in the Community' with Ron Wylie of Aston Villa FC.

He became acting Deputy Head Teacher.

Alan took early retirement to pursue other interests and began to write books for children and adults.

He has been a musician since the age of fourteen and still plays at weekends with his Oompah band.